"THERE'S ALWAYS ROOM IN MY BOUDOIR FOR COMPANY," FARGO SAID, OPENING HIS BEDROLL.

"I'm sure glad. I wouldn't have wanted to miss you, Fargo," Frannie said, joining him.

He felt her bare thigh press against his, the thrill quivering all through him. "I'll be taking you up on that," he said. He let his eyes move to the large firm breasts and down the length of her curved, creamy body.

"You like to tease, don't you?" Frannie murmured, closing her eyes.

"I like to have fun." In an instant he was tracing his fingers along her body. . . .

Exciting Westerns by Jon Sharpe

THE TRAILSMAN

27

BLOODY
HERITAGE

by
Jon Sharpe

A SIGNET BOOK
NEW AMERICAN LIBRARY

PUBLISHER'S NOTE

This novel is a work of fiction. Names, characters, places, and incidents either are the product of the author's imagination or are used fictitiously, and any resemblance to actual persons, living or dead, events, or locales is entirely coincidental.

NAL BOOKS ARE AVAILABLE AT QUANTITY DISCOUNTS
WHEN USED TO PROMOTE PRODUCTS OR SERVICES.
FOR INFORMATION PLEASE WRITE TO PREMIUM MARKETING DIVISION,
NEW AMERICAN LIBRARY, 1633 BROADWAY,
NEW YORK, NEW YORK 10019.

Copyright © 1984 by Jon Sharpe

The first chapter of this book appeared in *Warpaint Rifles*, the twenty-sixth volume of this series.

SIGNET TRADEMARK REG. U.S. PAT. OFF. AND FOREIGN COUNTRIES
REGISTERED TRADEMARK—MARCA REGISTRADA
HECHO EN CHICAGO, U.S.A.

SIGNET, SIGNET CLASSIC, MENTOR, PLUME, MERIDIAN and NAL BOOKS
are published by New American Library,
1633 Broadway, New York, New York 10019

First Printing, March, 1984

1 2 3 4 5 6 7 8 9

PRINTED IN THE UNITED STATES OF AMERICA

The Trailsman

Beginnings . . . they bend the tree and they mark the man. Skye Fargo was born when he was eighteen. Terror was his midwife, vengeance his first cry. Killing spawned Skye Fargo, ruthless, cold-blooded murder. Out of the acrid smoke of gunpowder still hanging in the air, he rose, cried out a promise never forgotten.

The Trailsman, they began to call him, all across the West: searcher, scout, hunter, the man who could see where others only looked, his skills for hire but not his soul, the man who lived each day to the fullest, yet trailed each tomorrow. Skye Fargo, the Trailsman, the seeker who could take the wildness of a land and the wanting of a woman and make them his own.

*The Wyoming Territory, early 1860s,
where the land was as wild as the men
who fought and died on it.*

1

In the crisp forenoon the tall broad-shouldered man with the lake-blue eyes rode the big black-and-white pinto up the long coulee and abruptly drew rein. Below him the lush meadow stretched to the creek lined with cottonwoods and alders. About halfway across, two canvas-topped wagons had halted, while toward them rode a half-dozen horsemen at full gallop.

Skye Fargo's eyes narrowed at those pushing riders. Something in the way they rode—loose in their saddles, red-faced, shouting as they forced their horses over the soft ground—told him they were bad news. Swiftly he drew the Ovaro back down the far side of the draw, dismounted and ground-hitched him, and in another moment had stationed himself in the protection of some chokecherry bushes from where he had a clear view of the scene below. The six riders were just yanking their sweating mounts to a jarring halt a few yards in front of the two wagons.

At that same moment a wiry, pigeon-breasted man wearing a derby hat, with gartered shirt-sleeves and bright red galluses, stepped down from the driver's seat of the lead wagon. Fargo was close enough to hear the loud greeting of the big lead rider on the steel-dust horse.

"Johnson, by God, if it ain't Mr. Kite Johnson himself in person!" And the barking laugh was instantly picked up by his companions, the roar of their high spirits sweeping up to the choke-cherry bushes where the Trailsman's lake-blue eyes had turned to blue quartz as he noted the handguns in tied-down leather, the Winchesters in their saddle scabbards and the loose arrogance with which the six sat their heaving animals. It was obvious that they'd been drinking.

"Johnson, come on over and greet your visitors," shouted a second rider, a man wearing a brown bandanna around his thick neck. He was standing up in his stirrups, scratching himself as he snapped out the words, his big orange-colored face gleaming with laughter. The other men joined his guffaw, yanking their horses' mouths unnecessarily, spitting, their eyes combing the wagons, which showed no signs of life other than the two teams of horses standing still, looking at the visitors. It suddenly crossed Fargo's mind that it might be a lynching.

The little man with the derby hat had just taken a step toward the six horsemen when Fargo's searching eyes caught a movement at the opening of the second wagon. It was a quick movement, yet clearly revealed a blond head of hair over a very pale face and a bare and thoroughly female arm and shoulder.

The roar that went up showed that the riders had seen it too.

"By God, Stacey, you told it right. We've struck gold," cried the man with the orange-colored face.

Stacey, the first speaker and obvious leader of the group, leaned forward on his saddle horn, his thick arms crossed. "Come on out, girls. You got company." Then, spitting over his horse's withers, he dropped his bloodshot eyes to the man named Kite Johnson. "Good boy, there, Kite. Good boy." And a great laugh rumbled out of him.

Kite Johnson had stepped away from the wagon, holding his arms well out from his waist to show that he was unarmed.

"You're Stacey, that right?" And Fargo caught the caution in the man's voice that was not quite fear.

"Mr. Kite Johnson, you better remember that. Dutch Stacey—remember it! Shit, Kite boy, you know me and my friends from last year when you brought your fucking auction and second-dealt me that cold-ass redhead with the one eye." And quick as a lick he drew the gun at his right hip and began firing at the ground right at Kite Johnson's feet.

The little man's narrow face turned ashen beneath the derby hat as he began to hop frantically out of the way of the bullets. Instantly the

11

other men drew their guns and joined the fun, roaring with laughter and calling out to the wagons as terrified female faces began to appear.

At the point where Kite Johnson was ready to drop, the men stopped firing, broke their guns and started to reload. Kite was drenched with sweat; his whole body was shaking. He barely managed to speak. "What do you want, Stacey? My God, man, I've always done right by you and your boys. How come all this? What do you want?"

"You know damn well what we want," shouted a man with a totally bald head. "We want that pussy you got loaded in those wagons. And right now!"

The group roared at this, their horses stamping now as they recovered their wind and picked up on the excitement. The teams that had been pulling the wagons, however, after looking over the newcomers, now dropped their heads to resume cropping the lush feed, harnesses jingling as they kicked at flies.

Fargo watched Kite Johnson making a tremendous effort to stay on his trembling legs, and finally the little man said, "You mean, you want to hold the auction out here?"

Stacey didn't answer him. "Get them women outside them wagons," he snapped. "We want to look 'em over."

Without turning his head, Johnson called out for the women to appear. He seemed to gather strength in giving the order.

Fargo's eyes brightened with curiosity while a roar of welcome sprang from the throats of the horsemen as some dozen women began to climb down from the two wagons. Fargo was surprised to see that they were young and some were even rather good-looking.

Kite Johnson repeated his question. "You want the auction now, then?"

Stacey grinned down from his big steel-dust horse. "Figured we would save all of us time and trouble with you not having to go through all that auctioneering business."

"No trouble," Kite said quickly, almost stammering as the visitors' plan began to unfold. "Hell, Stacey, I been running my auctions six, seven years now. Always offer the best product and never had no complaints. These lovely women"—and Fargo caught the purr that entered his voice as he stepped into his role— "why they come from far away as Boston, Philadelphia. Good families. San Francisco, that little girl over there; and that young lady with the red hair, her family, one of the fanciest in Chicago. I go to a whole lot of trouble collecting these brides-to-be for this woman-starved country, let me assure you." Kite Johnson had suddenly swept right out of his fear and timidity, and supported by his thoroughly rehearsed pitch, he seemed even to increase in size and certainly, so Fargo noted, in vibration. He was almost quivering with energy as he extolled the virtues of his ". . . young ladies from the very best families, who would make any red-blooded man a wife and mother of his children of which he would forever be proud. Why, if I say so myself, do you know any other such benefactor who finds young ladies good, virile husbands, and for you pioneering Americans, strong-loined wives? Who else, I say, offers such a prime, essential service? And at small remuneration to myself, let me add."

Dutch Stacey and his friends were chuckling with real pleasure at the performance, and now, as Kite paused in his peroration, Stacey's big head began wagging from side to side.

"Kite, boy . . . forget the auction. We are here so's we can cut all that bullshit and just like skim off some of the cream. You understand?"

Kite Johnson's face turned red, then gray at the thought of the ruination of his auction. "But I won't have enough left for an auction if you men bid on them here—I mean, like when we get to Washing Springs."

"Kite, my friend, you don't get me even yet. There ain't going to be no auction, no bidding. We are just, like, helping ourselves."

The charged pause fell like a knife into the tableau, and for several moments Kite, the women, the six riders and even the horses, it seemed, waited in a quivering silence in the gleaming meadow.

"That will ruin me," Kite Johnson said softly.

"Tough."

"And it'll ruin my girls."

"Fuck the girls."

14

"And by God, ain't that the idea," roared someone, and the whole group joined his wild laughter.

Meanwhile the girls were out of the wagons and had lined up behind Kite, their "benefactor." Fargo had a clear view of them. They were tense, fearful; yet with some, the moment seemed to emphasize certain aspects that he found attractive—fear sharpened them, changed their usual tempo, showed in one's defensive posture, in another's defiance or even in a pleading look, each reacting in her own way to the bizarre moment.

Stacey was leaning partly out of his saddle, holding his hand out toward one of the riders, who was passing a bottle. "Kite, you and me just know those girls never seen any town east of the Mississippi nor west of the Tetons. You're full of shit with that Boston, 'Frisco talk!" He grabbed the bottle, tilted it into his jaws, allowing some to run down his chin and into his shirt. Gasping, he passed it back, easy, laughing. And suddenly the gun was in his hand and he wasn't laughing any longer.

"The boys will look over the merchandise and tell Harold here which one they're wanting." And he threw his thumb at the man with the brown bandanna and orange-colored face.

"I want that one on the end," a tall, narrow-faced man said.

"So do I," Harold barked, glaring at the man who had spoken.

15

Stacey was chuckling, the six-gun still in his hand. "Wrong. Both you fellers got it wrong. That one is Stacey's." And he grinned, revealing a gap where two lower teeth were missing.

Fargo's eyes had spotted the young girl standing slightly apart from the others. She stood defiantly, her head thrown back, her full bosom high and clearly outlined beneath the tight shirt. She wore tight trousers, and his eyes slipped over her loins and legs admiringly, saw that she was a lot more than curvaceous; she had an air, a sparkle in her eyes, a grace when she made even the slightest move. Her dark brown hair, swept back from a high, full forehead, emphasized widely spaced eyes. And her mouth was wide, the lips full and mobile. She was, he decided, damned good-looking.

The other men were rapidly announcing their preferences and a couple of arguments were brewing.

"How about some bids to settle it?" Kite Johnson, stepping back into his auctioneer role, made one more attempt to salvage the financial wreckage.

Fargo's instinct, that inner voice he knew so well, was ringing through him. It was the instinct that had saved him more times than he could count: an animal, feeling thing, of nature, certainly part of his Cherokee heritage. And it called him now.

He saw her start to move even before she could have known it herself, her body tightening;

16

a kind of charge seemed to suffuse her. And he was already bounding back over the lip of the coulee, grabbing the Ovaro's reins, stepping into the saddle, and all in a single, singing movement was up and racing over the top of the rise, the shouts tearing up from the men below as the girl ran toward the wagons. Nobody seemed to notice the big man galloping down on the big black-and-white horse. The girl was just reaching the nearest wagon, her hair flying, with the riders nearly on top of her.

Fargo, kicking the Ovaro into a super effort, suddenly let out a bloodcurdling scream that sounded as though an entire tribe of Indians was on the attack. And it served its purpose. The paralyzing shock it brought gave him the seconds he needed as he charged into their midst. With the barrel of his .45 he struck Harold across his back, knocking him right out of his saddle, and without a break in rhythm, slammed Dutch Stacey on his gun arm. A third man was just lifting his own handgun to fire when Fargo, not close enough to strike him, pulled the trigger of the big Navy Colt. The bullet, smashing into the rider's shoulder, spun him in his saddle, and he fell, screaming more with rage than pain in a tangle of reins and curses while his horse, shorn of its rider, swept on.

The girl had reached the wagon and was about to pull herself up as Fargo, swerving the Ovaro, reached down to grab her, the other riders almost on top of him. Desperately, the girl tried to pull away, not realizing he wasn't one of the gang, but his grip was secure as he seized her under the arms and dragged her up and across the pommel of his saddle. Her shirt ripped almost completely in two, and one snow-white breast sprang almost into his face as he shoved her facedown across his horse, while she kicked and screamed in rage, trying to turn to rake her nails across his eyes.

"Goddammit, I'm trying to help you," he snapped at her. But she was too far gone in her fear and fury to listen, as he turned the big horse, smashing the Colt this time at a rider who had fired so close to his head he felt the heat of the bullet passing with only the width of a playing card between himself and death. Reaching down, he grabbed the rider's boot, yanked with all his strength and unseated him, flipping him over the other side of his horse.

The effort almost cost Fargo his own balance and he came within an ace of losing the girl, only just managing to keep her on the horse by grabbing her between her legs and pinning her. With his big hand reaching into her crotch from the rear, he held her fast, his fingers and palm tight as steel on her anus and vagina.

She kept trying to kick, but his crotch hold allowed only small movements of her legs. When she bit his leg, he tightened his grip like a vise while she screamed curses at him.

For an instant she was coherent, screaming, "You fucking bastard."

"Relax and enjoy it, honey. Too bad you've got these damn trousers on."

He had turned the big pinto and now they raced back across the meadow and up the long slope down which he had ridden only moments before. Shots cut the air all around them, but surprise and the decisiveness of each of the Trailsman's moves had given him the advantage as the gang lined out in pursuit, the big Ovaro, even while carrying a double load, stretching the distance.

Fargo knew it couldn't last. Even the Ovaro couldn't keep up such a pace. But he had already made his plan, and in a matter of moments, with shots still cutting too close, with the girl raging under his determined grip, they reached the top of the slope and raced down into the draw, straight toward a stand of cottonwoods he'd ridden through hardly more than half an hour before.

In a moment they reached the clearing he was looking for, where sometime previously several cottonwood trees had been cut down, leaving stumps about three feet high near a stream of water. Evidently a freshet had later occurred, washing a number of fallen logs against the stumps, and so formed a small angle, making an ideal breastwork from which to fire.

"Jump," Fargo shouted at the girl, releasing her, while he swept out of the saddle and the big horse sped on into the trees. He landed beside the girl in a mass of debris, fully protected by the logs.

In seconds the riders broke into the clearing, but Fargo had pulled the Sharps down with him and, rolling now, had come up under perfect cover, knocking the first man right out of his saddle. With the girl beside him, he found another target, the gang's bullets wasted as Fargo and the girl dug into their redoubt. In the next instant they saw it was over. The Trailsman had them dead in his sights. They drew rein, throwing down their guns, their arms lifted.

"All right, mister." Dutch Stacey snarled the words, his face twisted in pain, holding his shattered arm as he sat his horse, glaring at Fargo. "I'll be seeing you again."

"Not unless you're damned unlucky," Fargo said mildly. But that mild tone was set in steel. "Now get your ass out of here. You're lucky I didn't get mad at you." The round barrel of the Sharps swept the group. "You can leave your guns."

They were gone in a moment. Fargo waited, listening, to be sure. Then he whistled for the Ovaro.

"I suppose I should thank you," the girl said stiffly as she stood up and stepped out of the log fort. "I didn't realize you weren't one of them."

"The pleasure was mine," Fargo answered, a smile touching his lips as she took a step and began to limp.

"Though from your behavior I don't see that you're really all that different," she shot at him.

"I'm worse," he shot back at her, and reached out his hand to help her.

"Just don't touch me."

"Not until you ask me—nicely." And he swept her angry face with a big grin.

She had pulled her torn shirt around her, yet her firm, springy breasts all but refused to be hidden to her great irritation as she began pulling and tucking to cover herself.

"You can ride back with me to the wagons."

"I'd rather walk!" she slashed at him.

"Suit yourself." He swung up onto the Ovaro and started to cross the clearing. Looking back, he watched her limping, her face set in determination. "Get up behind and sit on the saddle skirt," he told her, turning the horse.

"No, thank you!"

He kneed the Ovaro and in a moment had grabbed her arm. "Get up like I say or I'll put you up the way I had you before." He looked straight down into glaring hazel eyes. "Take my hand and then pull yourself up and over. It's easy."

She hesitated, tried another painful step, and said, "I suppose I have to, dammit!"

"We'll be moving fast; you better hold on to me."

"I'll see if I have to."

He grinned at the disgust she put into her voice as she settled herself on the saddle skirt behind the high cantle. "You'll have to, honey."

21

"Then the pleasure will be all yours."

Fargo's grin broadened. "Say, that's one for you."

In a few moments they reached the wagons. There was no sign of Stacey and his companions. The girls were standing around Kite Johnson, waiting to see what had happened.

"Thank God you're all right." Kite Johnson helped the girl down from the pinto, then offered his hand to Fargo. "I could use a drink. How about yourself?"

"Good enough. I'll take some water." The girls eyed the broad shoulders and big chest in open admiration as he loosened the pinto's cinch, slipped the bit out of his mouth.

"Mister, you wouldn't be heading for Washing Springs, would you?"

"I might be, honey." Fargo grinned at the short, green-eyed blonde with the large pillowy bosom and sparkling mouth.

"My name's Frannie." Her frank eyes looked at him with a childlike friendliness.

"Glad to meet you, Frannie."

"I'm Kite Johnson," the wiry entrepreneur said, cutting in. "It'd be real good if you rode on in with us. It ain't far to the Springs, but those boys might take it in mind to come back."

Fargo was looking at the girl, who had moved toward Frannie and was testing her weight on her injured ankle.

"Sally, you all right?" the blonde asked.

"I'm all right. I think it just twisted. Nothing broken. It'll be all right."

"You don't know how lucky you are. It would have been awful with those ugly men."

"I don't think I had much choice." Her tone was sour.

Fargo's grin spread across his face. "I like your way with the humor," he said.

The girl looked at him and said nothing.

"Say, you didn't tell us your name," Frannie said.

"That's right, I didn't."

"Well, what is it?" she prodded, laughing, and swayed slightly in his direction.

He could feel the heat coming from her and his own desire suddenly rising.

"Fargo," he said, "Skye Fargo." And at the words he felt the girl Sally stiffen. The surprise was still in her face when he looked directly at her.

She regained her composure instantly. "I might have known." Her voice was soft, wry, almost as though she was speaking to herself. "Skye Fargo, the Trailsman."

"Something I can do for you, honey?"

"That depends."

"On what?"

"I've been looking for you."

The grin spread all over Fargo's face. "You dealt them, honey, now bet 'em."

2

Night had long since fallen over the sleeping camp when Fargo pushed back the unruly black hair that fell over his forehead and lifted himself away from Frannie as she unlocked her legs from around his waist, and rolled over onto his back. His eyes were half closed as he looked up contentedly into the high night sky.

Frannie let a sigh come from deep inside her. "God, Fargo, that was really special."

"Isn't it always, honey?" He rose up on an elbow and looked down into milky green eyes, wet, parted lips, feeling her breath on his face. In the light of the moon she was clearly visible. He let his eyes move down the length of her curved, creamy body, the large firm breasts with the nipples long and thick, the pink circles wide around each. Slowly he traced his finger around each nipple, then down between the delicious mounds, slipping along her long body, still damp with perspiration, as he smelled the marvelous odor of their long tussle in his bedroll mixing ineffably with the smells of pine and hemlock.

"There's more where that came from," she murmured, closing her eyes in ecstasy at his touch. He watched the corners of her mouth twitching.

"I'll be taking you up on that," he said, and lay back down again, looking up once more at the great starry sky.

Nearby a horse nickered and he heard the casual whiffle of the pinto who was picketed in close. And Fargo reflected at the wonderful surprise of her coming to him just like that, walking in on him as he was climbing into his bedroll, clad only in his shorts. She had stood there in surprise, it seemed to him, staring at his bare chest.

And she'd said, "If it works out with the auction, this time tomorrow I'll have me a husband, a man I will never have seen before."

Fargo hadn't hesitated. There was something quite singular, something very direct and honest in her, and certainly a tremendous willingness. Now as she dozed beside him his thoughts ran back over the day.

Following the action with Dutch Stacey and his boys, he had traveled with the wagons, riding point much of the time, checking the drag, always covering the trail closely for sign. The Trailsman's job was to see, not just to look the way most did, noticing only the obvious. He read the land as though it were a book. It was his love; the feel, the very breath of the great country.

There were no signs that they were either being followed or set up for an ambush ahead.

"Figure the liquor wore off on the boys right fast, do you?" Kite Johnson had suggested.

"Appears so." The Trailsman had squinted into the westering sunlight. "We'll make camp up there by the tableland," he'd said.

Kite Johnson had nodded, his jaws working fast as he chewed on some cutplug. "Can't be too careful."

Fargo hadn't answered but had kicked the Ovaro ahead to get away from the little man's need for idle chatter.

All the way to Washing Springs he had waited for Sally to speak to him after her surprising announcement, but she hadn't appeared and he assumed she must be resting her twisted ankle. He saw her only at supper and had found her eyes on him across the cookfire, but when he'd returned her gaze she'd looked away. Let her take her time, come to him when she was ready. Or not. In any case he had his own search. It was what had brought him into this part of the country on yet another false lead. But he was used to finding a cold trail in his long hunt for the murderers of his father and mother and young brother. He had found one of the trio already— one less killer in the world. He'd get the other two and make sure they knew who he was before their last moment. It was just a matter of time, of when and where.

"What're you thinking about?" the girl beside him suddenly asked, and he felt her bare thigh press against his, the thrill quivering all the way through him.

"Tell me about this auction business," he said.

"Not much to tell that you don't know already. Kite finds the girls, gets them to sign a contract with him, then brings them out to the territory and auctions them off to be wives to women-starved men."

"Bit like a cathouse on the hoof, isn't it?"

Frannie's small laugh was all humor. "It could look that way. But most of them actually do get married. Or, so I've heard." She sighed. "Guess I'll find out."

"I can see how they'd want wives," Fargo conceded. "There isn't a whole lot to pick from out in this part of the country, except now and again one of the sporting girls passing through."

"A lot of men don't want that kind for anything permanent," Frannie said. "I've a kind of feeling Kite's pretty much on the square. You know, in a way he could be doing a good thing."

Fargo turned his head to look at the side of her face. "You looking for a husband? I don't see you as that lonesome."

"If you'd lived in a place like Willow Falls, you'd be looking for anything," she said sourly. "You can die in a place like that and chances are nobody'd know the difference."

Fargo grinned, liking her sharp humor. "Willow Falls? I thought you were from Boston or New York or Philadelphia," he said, imitating Kite Johnson's patter. "Gee, I'm disappointed."

"Well, Kite does lay it on. Mostly the girls come from places like the Falls or maybe something as fancy as St. Joe or some such. Hell, don't you know that men like to be fooled, Fargo?"

"Don't you know that women *insist* on being fooled!"

She was silent a moment and then said, "Doesn't matter, long as it's nice is how I look at it."

A softness in her tone caught him and he touched her lightly. "So tomorrow he'll hold the auction and you'll get yourself a husband."

"Maybe."

"Want to bet on it?"

"Nope."

"What about Sally? I think she's got other plans on her mind."

"What makes you say that?" And he caught the suspicion in her tone.

"She seems different."

Suddenly Frannie sat up, clasped her arms around her knees, dropped her head down and turned to look at the big man. "Shit, Fargo, you like her? Here we just got through lovemaking and you're thinking of someone else."

"Cut it out. I asked you a simple question. Answer it straight or don't answer it at all. But cut that damn shit."

"I was just funning a little."

"I don't go for that jealous stuff."

"I take it back!" She swung round abruptly, her naked breasts bouncing against his arm, her hands wide open in an offering gesture. "I don't like jealous men either." She was suddenly teasing, breathing her words hard. And now her eyes fell to his wide chest, the firm pectoral muscles that gleamed beneath the smooth skin, almost shining in the moonlight. Her eyes dropped further. "That how you got that—from a jealous woman?" The tip of her tongue was showing between her lips as she reached out and touched the half-moon-shaped scar on the top of his forearm.

"Got that from a grizzly. A mistake on my part that I won't make again."

"I gather you handled the situation well enough, or you wouldn't be here to tell about it."

"That's the size of it."

She was leaning closer to him. "I'm sure glad. I wouldn't have wanted to miss you, Fargo."

He was silent.

"Fargo . . ."

She was running her forefinger over the scar. "I'm really not the jealous sort. I just—like you a lot."

"I think you are the jealous sort," he said, and he watched the pout come to her lips.

"I take back what I said. I'm not jealous. So help me God! I've never been jealous in my entire life and I never will be! I swear on a dozen Bibles!" She was wagging her head, hardly containing her laughter, and now he joined her, suddenly poking his finger into her bare ribs.

"I'm not ticklish!"

"I think you are!"

And in an instant he had her on her back, his fingers racing like raindrops over her quivering body as she could no longer hold her laughter. She tried in vain to tickle him back, but he was immune. Now they were both roaring with laughter as they romped over his bedroll, panting and heaving and gasping together until he suddenly spread her on her back and drove his enormous member right up into her as she cried out in ecstasy. Together they rode until the exquisite moment when their thrashing loins reached the ultimate, gasping, moaning, crying climax, she enveloping his entire maleness which he drove into her like a tree—high, deep and throbbing until they exploded, absolutely together.

They lay supine, damp and limp with satiation.

It was awhile before she spoke in his ear. "I'd better get going and get my beauty sleep, so I can be in good condition for the auction."

"So long, then. And good luck tomorrow."

"I'll need it."

He closed his eyes and lay very still, taking in the night sounds, feeling suddenly the cool stirring of a random wind on his face and hands. He felt the change in the atmosphere before his ears caught the tiny crack of the dry branch.

In one sweeping motion he was up on one knee away from his bedroll, the big Navy Colt in his hand.

"It's only me. Sally."

30

"About time," he said as she walked into the little clearing.

"I didn't mean to invade your boudoir, but I saw that your company had left." Disapproval etched her words.

"There's always room in my boudoir for more company," he said amiably. "Come on in." He stood up, clad only in his shorts. The moon, which had been behind a wisp of cloud, now came out full force and he watched her looking at his bare chest. Catching herself, she tore her eyes away.

"Cooler like this, especially when I'm trying to get some sleep." And he sat down on the edge of his bedroll, crossing his legs. "Have a seat."

She looked around, refusing to join him on his bedding, and seated herself on the ground, her knees tucked underneath her. She was wearing trousers, a man's white shirt. And he realized that even a potato sack wouldn't be able to hide the lines of her full figure.

"Sorry to bother you at this late hour," she went on crisply. "Only I have to talk to you. There was no time during the day with everybody around, and I needed to keep off my ankle. And then, this evening, well, I hope I haven't come at a wrong moment." Her tone was acid.

"Lady, tell me what you want."

He could feel the irritation running through her body and imagined her face reddening, though he couldn't actually see it that clearly in the moonlight.

31

"Very well, Mr. Fargo, I will get to the point. I want you to find my father, John Logan." The clear outline of her features grew indistinct now as a light cloud moved across the moon.

"I thought you were looking for a husband," Fargo speared at her.

She lowered her head, looking down at her hands lying on her lap. Without looking up at him she spoke. "I signed up with Kite under false pretenses. I simply didn't have the money to get out here. It was my only chance." She looked up at him. "I couldn't possibly go through with such a thing."

"And what about the auction? Kite isn't going to take kindly to being double-crossed. Or if you go through with it, what the hell are you going to tell the damn fool who bids for you; or will you just run out on him?"

Her brows knit, and she looked down at her hands again. "I plan to tell Kite. I'm going to talk to him in the morning. I'll pay him back somehow, someday." She lifted her eyes toward him as the moon shone clearly now. "Look, you understand, don't you? I have to find my father." She stopped, added, "I'm not basically a dishonest person. I'll pay Kite back."

"You don't have to convince me, honey. And anyway, I don't know that I'm so sure about your honesty."

"Just what do you mean!" she flung at him. "That's not fair! You don't know me. You don't know me at all!"

"I know your kind," he said equably.

"My kind!"

"Stuck up. Dishonest. You think all you've got to do is smile and wave your ass at Kite Johnson and he'll roll over."

"I don't think anything of the kind!" She stood up, almost tripping on a root but not actually losing her balance. "I'm sorry I bothered you, Mr. Fargo. Perhaps we'd best just forget it!"

The grin spread all over Fargo's face. "I wondered how important it was to you to find your father."

He thought she was going to stamp her foot, but she only clenched her fists at her sides and fought for control. "You win. I hope I passed your test." She stood before him, her breath coming in spurts. "Will you or will you not help me find my father?" Her tone was glacial.

"Sit down."

He thought she was going to refuse and he was about to tell her to go to hell, but suddenly she sat again.

"Start at the beginning and tell me the whole thing. Don't leave anything out, and . . ." He let the pause fall meaningfully. "And don't try lying. I can always tell."

He watched her controlling herself again and had the urge to tell her she was getting better at it, but refrained. And suddenly it came together, the rigidity, the snappy way she spoke, her sharp gestures. "You're a schoolteacher, aren't you?"

"Yes, Mr. Fargo, I am a schoolteacher. Now, do you want to hear what I have to say?"

"Shoot?"

"I don't really know for certain that my dad's out here," she began. "He left home—back in Missouri—almost ten years ago. About a year after he left, we—my mother—got a letter from him, from Washing Springs. She wrote him, three letters I think in the following years, and never received an answer." She paused, taking a deep breath. Fargo's eyes touched her swelling bosom.

"I was born and brought up in Willow Falls," Sally went on. "Yes, I am a schoolteacher, or was until—this. Mother told us that Dad came out to Wyoming to find a better place for us, to make a stake was how she put it." She picked up a twig, snapped it between her fingers. "It wasn't easy in Willow Falls. Frannie can tell you that. Maybe she did." Fargo caught the tightening in her voice.

"So that left just you and your mom?"

"And Danny, my younger brother."

"Was there anything in your father's letter that would suggest what happened to him, why he never wrote again?"

"All he said was he missed us and loved us and had fallen onto a good thing, and would be sending for us soon. And that was nine years ago." She was shaking her head. "I've never been able to understand it. Why would he just disappear like that?"

"Maybe he's dead," the Trailsman said

bluntly. "I'm sorry, but you have to look at all the possibilities, and I'm sure you've already thought of that."

"Yes, I have thought of it. Maybe he is. Maybe he is dead."

"How come you decided at this particular time to come looking for him?"

"My mom died six months ago."

"And where is your brother?"

"I left Danny with friends. He's pretty grown up for his age."

"But what made you come on out? Not just your mother's dying."

"I'd thought about it while she was still alive—often. I even wrote to the marshal's office in Washing Springs. The man who wrote back said he'd never heard of any John Logan. But the thing was, the attitude my mom had. I mean, it was strange. She was funny about it."

"How—funny?"

"Whenever Danny or I brought him up, Mom would start talking about something else. She never initiated any conversation about him. He might as well have been dead."

"So when your mother died, you decided to come and see if you could find him."

"I wrote another letter to the marshal at Washing Springs."

"Did you get an answer?"

She nodded wearily. "It was a different marshal. I forget the name. He said he had nothing to tell me. He had never heard of anyone named John Logan, and that was that."

"Could I see your father's letter?"

"I don't have it. I think Mother destroyed it." She paused, clenching and unclenching her hand. "There was one thing she did mention once—and never brought up again."

"What was that?"

"She said Dad had written that he was working at a place called Hangtown."

"Hangtown? Did she say where it was?"

"No, and I tried to find it on some maps but couldn't."

"So you decided to come anyway."

"I decided to come anyway. I began to think something bad might have happened to him. I don't know. Maybe it's all foolishness, but I felt I owed it to myself, maybe to my mother and Danny, or even to my father. I don't know. I don't know. I have tried living with it but decided I don't want to leave unfinished business."

"And you're a schoolteacher," Fargo said, his voice kindly. "Neat, tidy life. Nothing left undone."

"It just seemed so strange his not writing after that one letter."

"Did your mother ever seem to feel he'd maybe met another woman? Or maybe gotten into some kind of trouble?"

"She never said so. Or—yes she did sort of hint

36

at it, that there might be another woman. But nothing direct."

"But if he wants to live a completely new life, why do you want to find him? I mean, if he doesn't want you and your brother. I'm sorry, I'm not trying to be cruel, but I have to get to the bare bones. You understand me?"

She nodded quickly. "Yes, I do."

"And so why do you still want to find him? Maybe he'd rather you didn't."

She looked at him, her head high, her jaw firm. "He's still my father. Will you help me find him? The man who told me about you said you were the best tracker there was, that you knew the country like you knew your own two hands."

"He was right."

"I'm afraid your modesty was one of the qualities he failed to mention," she said, cool again, her lips thin.

Fargo grinned. "I'm expensive, Miss Logan."

"How much?"

"This kind of job is two thousand dollars."

"That's too much money."

"How do you gauge that?"

"By my pocketbook."

"I thought your pocketbook didn't have anything since you cheated Kite Johnson to get a free ride out here."

"I haven't cheated him—yet. And the reason I did what I did was so I'd have some money for expenses like yourself, only I cannot possibly afford two thousand dollars."

37

"Make me an offer."

She seemed to be studying him. Then she said, "Five hundred—now. And more if he's still alive and you find him."

"You mean you'll be open to further negotiation."

"Yes. I don't know what we might find. But I am being straight with you. I do have some more savings at home, if I need it. And I'll pay you. I'm not trying to get you cheap or anything like that."

He stood up. "I'll take the money now," he said.

"Very well." She rose and, reaching into her trouser pocket, brought out an envelope. "There's five hundred dollars in there," she said. "All that I have."

"Pretty sure of yourself," he said, admiring the sudden frankness she was showing.

"It's all I have."

The moon was even brighter as the last vestige of cloud moved away and the little clearing was flooded with light, almost like day.

Fargo's glance dropped to the girl's waist where her shirt had ridden up from her belt and was billowing out slightly, but was taut as a drumhead over the twin points of her upturned breasts. He let his eyes move down to the slight swell at her belly just at her belt, feeling the stirring in his loins.

"Have a good look," she snapped. "Mr. Fargo, our deal is a business deal and nothing but a business deal. Do you understand me?"

He grinned, aware that while she was looking at his face, her peripheral vision was still on the big flat muscles of his bare chest and shoulders, his belly, and as far down as his white shorts. "Kite Johnson's going to be hard to convince that you're not a necessary attraction for his auction tomorrow."

"That will be my business, Fargo. Not yours."

"I should mention to you that while I have accepted your five hundred, it's on account, depending on what I run into."

"That is the way I understood it."

"Also I want a completely free hand. No interference."

"And I accept that condition. I also have a condition, however."

"What's that?"

"*I* want no interference. You can have a free hand. But you keep your free hands to yourself!"

Fargo threw back his head and laughed.

"I mean what I say."

"Got'cha. But for now, why don't you just slow down and wait till you're asked?"

She said something, but half under her breath, and he couldn't tell what it was. It sounded like "bastard." And then she turned away and was gone.

3

The pale, lemon-colored sun had just reached the center of the dusty blue sky. Inside the big tent Kite Johnson climbed onto the long trestle bar. A roar went up from the crowd, which numbered close to eighty men. There were no women, and the male customers, who had been eagerly awaiting the arrival of the little entrepreneur, had generously sampled the liquid refreshment brought out from town. Marshal Clyde Greenough had definitely refused a permit for Kite Johnson's auction within the precincts of Washing Springs and had banished the activity to the outskirts. "This here's a moral town," he had said gravely. "We got women, children to think about. Yup, I know they're gettin' married, and bein' a man of experience I understand the situation, and I sympathize. But the women and children and even some of the older men, they see it otherwise."

Thus, the marshal, a bony figure held together by a tight skin not only the color but texture of whang leather—in the Trailsman's estimation—

delivered his proclamation shortly before the arrival of Kite Johnson.

Fargo had arrived early, eager to see if anything might turn up on John Logan in the casual, often tipsy-sounding conversations that were inevitable at such gatherings. He was also eager to see the auction.

The tent was filled with bidders and non-bidders, all sharing the same interest; the need for excitement paramount even in the dullest old codger as it was in the youngest of the callow youths who lurked at the tent doorway to get a glimpse of the "merchandise from back East."

Right now Fargo's interest, along with everyone else's, was turned on the natty little man with red galluses and silvery white garters on his sleeves, who was holding up both hands to gentle the crowd.

"Quiet, gents; quiet if you please."

Perhaps Kite had waited too long to start the proceedings, Fargo wondered, for all at once a heavily bearded, greasy, malodorous man with very thick red hands, and with by now as much whiskey as blood in his veins, roared out belligerently, "Quit stallin' and bring out them women, Shorty, or you ain't gonna be able to!"

There was a loud murmur of impatient agreement with this hint of mayhem, and Fargo adjusted himself at the bar to be sure of a clear view of everything going on. He had already noted the presence of a great many guns in the crowd; he was also wondering how Sally Logan had managed with Johnson. Had she told him she didn't want to go through with the auction? Fargo had only seen her briefly early that morning on their way into Washing Springs. After arrival, Kite had kept the girls out of view to heighten the interest of the prospective bidders.

"Now don't go getting all worked up and ornery, boys," the little man was saying hurriedly. "I only want to put in one word; the women are coming right out, and kindly do not squeeze or handle them if you ain't got the money to make a bid. These are high-class ladies and it makes them nervous to be horsed with if a man ain't backing it up with a firm offer. I mean, these girls are all from good families, and I have spent time, money, nervous aggravation even, collecting them for the benefit of you young men. Now, any of you with serious intentions can get ready to bid!"

He stopped abruptly, wiped his mouth with the back of his hand and jumped down from the bar, accompanied by a roar of applause.

Fargo had been searching the crowd for Dutch Stacey or any of his boys but they were not present. Then, just as Kite Johnson strode to a curtained-off room at the rear of the tent Stacey, Harold and two other men walked in. Almost immediately their eyes found Fargo, who simply looked back at them until they turned away.

Only a few moments had passed while the crowd eagerly awaited Kite Johnson's return, and now he came back into the tent proper, leading twelve women, most of whom Fargo recognized. The room was still as a stone as Kite lined the women behind the bar, from which, at this point, no drinks were being served. Fargo suddenly realized that Sally Logan was not there. He looked over at Stacey and Harold to see their reaction but their faces were impassive.

Kite scrambled up onto the bar, faced the tent full of men and said nothing. He simply waited, allowing the excitement to build. Somebody sneezed, and the slender entrepreneur spoke.

"All right, Billie Ann. You're first." Kite peered down at a girl of about thirty, blond, slightly faded, but she wore a bright smile on her face as she stepped up onto the bar to stand beside her mentor.

Suddenly a middle-aged, black-bearded and tremendously hairy man, standing not far from Fargo, let out a roar. "Boys, if that ain't the prettiest white woman I ever seen!" And jerking out a pair of .44s from worn holsters, he shouted, "I bid one hundred dollars!" His beard snapped shut with his big jaws on those words and now his narrow eyes covered the room. "And don't a one of you bid agin' me, neither!" he added.

But a man on the other side of the tent either didn't hear this last remark or chose simply to ignore it. "One hundred and twenty-five dollars!" he bellowed.

The hairy man took a step toward this challenge, his face dark with rage. The crowd opened as if by magic, allowing free access for flying lead between the two men. "You buy yourself another woman, you little short-peckered bastard; this one's mine!"

"The hell she is!" The second bidder then made the mistake of reaching for his gun, obviously blind to the fact that the man with the big black beard already had his two in hand. It was his final mistake. He fell dead to the floor, a round bullet hole neatly between his gray eyes.

The tent was silent. Kite Johnson, apparently not unused to such goings-on, waited an appreciable length of time as death became a factor, and then resumed in a fresh voice. "If someone will kindly remove the gentleman before he gets trampled on, then we can proceed. . . ."

But all at once another bid was heard. It was the man who had yelled at Kite to hurry up and get on with the auction, the greasy man with the thick red hands. "I bid a hundred and a half!" At the same time he whipped out his six-guns, beating his surprised rival for Billie Ann's affections to the draw by a fraction of a second. It was a fraction as good as an hour. And Billie Ann went for one hundred and fifty dollars.

Both bodies removed, the auction proceeded, albeit with much invective and boiling emotion in the tent. Fargo was glad to see that Frannie went to a young man roughly her own age, although he was pretty drunk, and it might be a question how he would view his purchase—costing him three hundred dollars, for the bidding was brisk—on the morning after.

It was late afternoon when the last young lady was auctioned off to a buffalo hunter. Kite Johnson's face was wreathed in smiles. He'd been in top form. At one point during the heat of the auction he had even leaned down toward Fargo to remark, "Wouldn't yourself be in the market for a beautiful young wife, Fargo? Better get in on it before they're all gone."

Fargo shook his head, grinned back at the little man, still wondering what had become of Sally Logan.

The final bid was not completed without drollery. The prize was Polly, brunette, shapely and—so said Kite—age twenty-two. As the auctioneer drew her up onto the bar to stand beside him she smiled coyly at the crowd and unexpectedly lifted her dress a few inches above her knees.

Kite Johnson hissed at her angrily, "Stop that! You ain't back in that goddamn Omaha cathouse. These hayseeds ain't used to naked women, so stop scaring 'em. Act decent, dammit!"

And from the crowd came remarks that such a brazen hussy would sure not be the kind a man could trust when he was away from the house. Thus the bidding for Polly was not brisk, and there was no shooting over her favors. Swiftly, Kite let her go to a hefty man with a jaw like an anvil who allowed as how Polly was worth a hundred dollars to him. And he explained to the men standing near him that, "Time I work that frisky little filly in the fields all day, 'sides cookin' me three squares and raising me a houseful of young-sters, she ain't gonna have the time for lifting her skirt exceptin' to me."

In all, two men had died in action and as far as Fargo could see Mr. Johnson had pocketed a pretty penny.

These thoughts were running through his mind as he walked slowly some distance behind Frannie and her "husband" until they entered Washing Springs' only hotel, the Buffalo Horn, an unpainted two-story frame building whose sign announced, "Food and Lodging for Man and Beast."

He paused now across from the hotel, in the shadow furnished by the walkway against the hot late afternoon sun, watching Kite Johnson step briskly into the Buffalo Horn. He was carrying a black satchel with him, in which no doubt were his generous profits, or, as he'd put it to Fargo the day before, his "travel and managerial expenses for the young ladies."

Suddenly a voice nearby said, "Interesting, wasn't it?" He turned toward a tall, carefully dressed man wearing a black broadcloth suit and highly polished Wellington boots, a man in his early forties with a big head under yellow hair and with a clean-shaven, hard, square jaw.

"I'm Tyson Titchener; saw you out at the auction."

"Skye Fargo."

"I know. You're the Trailsman. If you're going

to be in town a while I've a proposition I'd like to put before you."

"I'll be staying at the Buffalo Horn," Fargo said, looking into the other man's slate-gray eyes.

"I'll be looking you up then." And with a nod of his big blond head, Tyson Titchener—who, Fargo noted, was carrying a hideout gun under his coat—nodded and walked on.

His eyes followed the other man along the street and out of sight. Gambler? Gunman? Whatever, Fargo sensed he was not a man to be fooled with.

Fargo's wide brow knitted now as he felt the sun warming the toes of his boots, and he looked over again at the Buffalo Horn. There was still no sign of Sally Logan.

Nor was there any news of a man named John Logan in the half-dozen saloons and eateries of Washing Springs. Fargo inquired of the barber, the undertaker, the blacksmith and the hostler at the O.K. Livery.

"It's a town that is finished, mister, since the mines shut down," an old-timer at the Good Times Saloon told him. "Folks can't be expected to recollect somebody maybe just passing through, maybe some eight, ten years ago."

And another had put it with equal clarity. "Hell, you are askin' about a man with two hands, two feet, two eyes and more'n likely two balls. What can I say? Could be anybody. People don't hang around this town. Who the hell'd want to?"

"He might've been a farmer," Fargo insisted.

"Mister, you close your eyes and just stand there and spit in this here saloon place and you'll hit a half-dozen farmers without even trying."

"No, they ain't no newspaper in Washing Springs. Over to Gebo, yes. But it's a now-and-again thing."

"Hangtown? Never heard of the place."

Fargo had insisted again. "It's supposed to be near Washing Springs."

"If it be, then it is six feet down, like a good many of the lawmen and nosy folk we've had around this here town."

When he'd walked into the marshal's office, Clyde Greenough was pouring a saucerful of milk for his black-and-tan cat. He put the saucer down carefully, talking to the animal, who totally ignored him, then walked over to his desk and sat down in a rickety wooden chair with an aged deer-hide seat.

"What kin I do for you, mister?" The wrinkled, leathery neck released the head sufficiently to allow a nod toward the only other chair in the tiny room, which, save for two spokes, had no back at all.

"I'm looking for a man who might have lived here, or at least in the country, could be awhile back. I know for a fact he was here ten years ago. Name of John Logan."

The marshal of Washing Springs was a bony man with big-knuckled hands and a cast in one eye, making it hard for people to know just where he was looking. He drew a plug of chewing tobacco from the pocket of his shirt and sliced off a generous portion with a clasp knife, one-handed, drawing the razor-sharp blade right up against his callused thumb. Holding the knife and tobacco in front of him, he considered his visitor, elbows on his desk, forehead raised beneath the brim of his dusty Stetson hat.

"You hunting bounty?"

"No, Logan's an old friend of mine."

"Can't help you. Never heard of any man name of Logan, though that don't mean much. Ten years, that is a good while. And we get a lot of comings and goings in Washing Springs."

He belched suddenly, without any change of expression on his guttered face, then carefully placed the cutplug deep inside his large jaws and began chewing, working up the taste. Presently, his words came around the chew as he said, "Anything else I can do for you?"

The Trailsman had been studying Clyde Greenough with exquisite care. It was his way to listen to the spaces between the words when a man spoke—to not be taken by the words but to probe the speaker's feelings. Thus he heard something in Clyde Greenough that caused him to take a second look at the marshal of Washing Springs. "Wonder if you might have any flyers around from the past few years. There's a chance he might be wanted by the law."

Clyde Greenough cut his good eye fast at his visitor at those words, his jaws worked faster, and leaning over, he spat directly into a tarnished brass cuspidor, getting some of the thick brown-and-yellow juice on the black-and-tan cat who had just come over to rub up for some more milk. "I'd know if there was, being as that's my job. And I never have seen anything like that." Then, catching the tightening look in Fargo's lake-blue eyes, he added, "You're welcome to study all of them," and he swept a long bony hand toward the wall across from his desk on which a great many flyers were affixed, some of them yellow from the passing years. "Got a description of him, have you?"

"Tall, I'd say in his forties."

"Got any special marking on him?" Greenough leaned back, tilting his chair onto its two rear legs but keeping his eyes directly on Fargo.

Fargo didn't even wait a beat. "He's got a long scar on the back of his right hand, an old one."

And as he spoke he watched Greenough, who didn't flicker an eye. But the Trailsman was also watching the marshal's breathing. He was sure Clyde Greenough had heaved a sigh of relief.

Marshal Greenough dropped his chair forward, bringing the front two legs down hard on the wooden floor. "You'll be helped by that," he said. "Those flyers always list such markings. You're welcome to go through them anytime, now or later." And he leaned over and spat again into the spittoon near his feet.

Fargo stood up. "I appreciate it, Marshal. I got some things to do right now, but maybe tomorrow I'll come by and take a look." He wanted to find the girl, for that inner voice was at him again. She couldn't have just disappeared without Kite Johnson wanting to know why.

"Good enough."

Fargo had walked to the door and now he turned, with his hand on the knob. "I've just got one more question. Don't take it personal. Who was marshal of Washing Springs before you?"

"I ain't taking it personal. Feller named Boden."

"He around?"

"He left the country awhile back."

Fargo bent down and stroked the cat, who was rubbing against his boot. "And any idea where he might be?"

Marshal Greenough's brow darkened. "You ask a helluva lot of questions, mister. And I'm sorry I'm just a dumb old country marshal who don't know the answers."

"Know a place named Hangtown?"

"Nope."

Fargo, seeing the glint in the other man's good eye and remembering how his breathing had relaxed at mention of a nonexistent scar on John Logan's hand, knew he had pushed it far enough. "Thank you for your time, Marshal. I'll come by tomorrow to take a look at those flyers then."

The marshal of Washing Springs leaned back in his chair, took off his Stetson hat and adjusted it at a fresh angle on his gray head. And said nothing.

Clearly, Clyde Greenough had been concerned that Fargo was looking for someone he didn't want him to find, and he'd been mighty relieved to hear of the scar. But who was it that the marshal feared Fargo was tracking? Was it anyone involved with John Logan?

The late afternoon sun was slanting down the mountain slopes, across the plain and into the dusty little town as Fargo started up the street. He heard someone calling his name and, turning, saw Frannie hurrying out of the Antelope Bar and Eatery.

"I saw you through the window!" The words came gasping out of her as she stood before him, red-faced, her eyes sparkling, her marvelous bosom thrusting at him. Fargo's thoughts instantly raced to the pleasures they had shared the night before, and he wondered where her future husband might be.

"I saw you," she repeated. "And I had to talk to you. What's happened to Sally? I know she talked to you."

"I have the same question," Fargo replied, thumbs in his belt and standing swing-hipped in front of the girl.

"She just disappeared," Frannie said, her green eyes round with astonishment.

"You haven't seen her since the auction?"

"Not since before. She told me she was going to talk to Kite, tell him she couldn't go through with it. And she wasn't with us when we came out to the tent." Frannie's eyes were darting up and down the dusty street as she spoke.

"I'll let you know if I find anything," Fargo said. He studied her a moment. "How's married life?"

"We're making it legal tomorrow." And then she added, wanly he thought, "I think."

"Good luck."

"Fargo . . ." The green eyes were soft, searching his face, her mouth slightly open.

"What can I do for you?"

"It was good last night."

"Well"—he grinned—"like a lady friend of mine just recently said, there's more where that came from."

"Is that a promise?"

"One way to find out."

"Fargo, I don't want to get married."

"Then don't."

"Miller Prouty—that's my fiancé—doesn't like to take no for an answer."

"I can't help you, honey."

Suddenly she was smiling. "I'll maybe find a way to help myself." And then just as suddenly she was frowning. "But I *am* worried about Sally."

"I'll see what I can dig up. I'm going to spend the night in town. If you maybe need me for anything . . ." he added, eyeing her speculatively.

"Where?"

"The Buffalo Horn."

"You got a room number?"

"I don't know it yet; I'm on my way to check in. But I'm sure you could find it if you wanted."

"I've got to get back." She had turned her head to look back at the Antelope Bar. "Miller is the jealous kind of man. I'll have to pass up tonight, Fargo. I mean . . ." She bit her lip. "Oh, shit!"

"Take care of yourself." Fargo paused. Then, "Look, you don't *have* to marry him, do you?"

He watched the tears standing in her eyes as she looked directly at him, shaking her head. Then, still without speaking, she turned and ran back to join Miller Prouty, whom she'd met only that afternoon.

Fargo followed her with his eyes. He was thinking how really terrible it must have been back in Willow Falls.

Before checking in at the Buffalo Horn, he took a walk down to the livery to see that the hostler was taking good care of the Ovaro. The hostler was an old man with only his lower teeth and whose neck was bent halfway down to his shoulder. He dragged one foot when he walked. One eye stuck much farther out of its socket than its companion, and he had difficulty speaking, croaking every now and then like a bullfrog. Birth—or maybe a horse? Fargo wondered.

"You taking good care of my horse?"

"Yup." Followed by a croak.

"I might be needing him in a hurry. You here all night?"

The old man nodded.

"What's your name?"

"Hank . . ."

Fargo checked the Ovaro, saw that he had feed and water. Then he slipped on his head stall, leaving the bit out of his mouth so he could feed. He threw on the blanket and saddled him, leaving the cinch loose so that if he were in a hurry, a quick pull would be all that was necessary.

He handed Hank a silver dollar. "You don't let anyone near my horse."

The old man nodded vigorously, croaking as he did so in affirmation.

Fargo's eyes fell on a stocky little buckskin, and suddenly he had a hunch. The girl could be in trouble. "I could be wanting an extra saddle horse. Buck there might do me."

"He's tough, good in the mountains, open country—both." Hank croaked several times at the conclusion of this information and began scratching himself vigorously in the crotch.

"Throw a regular stock saddle and bridle on him. I'll pay for him starting now."

The old man nodded, croaking as he dragged himself toward a saddle and bridle on a wooden bar by the door of the barn.

"You know where Hangtown is?"

The old hostler looked at him blankly, his Adam's apple pumping twice in his skinny throat. He said nothing.

It was just getting to be dusk as Fargo walked into the lobby of the Buffalo Horn. A shiny bald head glowed behind the desk, and as Fargo approached two cold eyes stared at him. Their owner was silent.

"The name is Fargo. Skye Fargo. I'll be needing a room for the night."

Those expressionless eyes glinted suddenly out of the rubbery red face. Then the head turned to survey the row of keys on the wall behind the desk and returned to address the big man with the bushy black hair, wide shoulders and lake-blue eyes.

"Your—uh—wife already took the room, mister. She'll be up there now, I reckon, since the key ain't here on the rack."

Fargo restrained the sour grin from showing on his face. Another point for the arrogant schoolteacher. Of course, it was the place to hide. But he didn't like some things coming too close. Damn her! Because she'd paid him five hundred dollars, she had a notion to play things her way.

"Mind telling me what room?"

"I don't mind. It's room number six."

With his long stride Fargo was quickly across the lobby and mounting the stairs, finding that he was relieved to discover where she was.

His footsteps made no sound on the old carpet and the building was silent save for a man's sudden barking laugh coming from one of the rooms as he passed. He wondered if it was one of Kite's customers with his new wife.

He paused a moment in front of number six, thinking to knock, but then deciding against it, he opened the door quickly and walked into the room.

He had a fleeting glimpse of a girl tied and gagged in the chair as the gun barrel smashed him across the legs and another blow behind his knees brought him to the floor. They were three, they were big and they were fast. They had him down on his back before the haze of pain in his legs faded enough for him to start kicking. Somebody was sitting on his chest, trying to get thumbs into his eyes. The Trailsman suddenly relaxed, went totally limp with a little cry of pain. At that instant there was a barely perceptible slackening in the drive of his attackers. It was enough. Swiftly Fargo twisted, brought a fist into the throat of the man sitting on him, elbowed another man wickedly in the crotch and, when the third man grabbed him around his chest in a bear hug, drove his chin against his attacker's ear and bored in with all the strength of his huge neck muscles. With a cry the man fell away. They were on him again. He kicked out, smashing one of his assailants in the kidney, the man releasing a grunt of agony. Then he drove the heel of his hand behind another man's skull right where it met his neck. There was no cry of pain; the man simply dropped to the floor. The third man was on his feet, reaching for his six-gun. Fargo's hand swept to his holster, but it was empty. They had seen to that. The other man had cleared leather, carrying up a big Navy Colt. Fargo's fingers continued down to draw the Arkansas throwing knife from the scabbard strapped to his right leg. As the shot rang out in the room the razor-sharp blade was already in the neck of the man with the gun. The bullet plowed harmlessly into the top of the wall next to the window.

His breath sawing, the Trailsman wasted no time in freeing the girl. It was suddenly evening and he lit the lamp to look at the three men, one of whom was dead, the other two unconscious. He didn't recognize any of them.

"That was sure a dumb thing to do," he said to Sally, revealed in sudden light.

"I'm sorry . . ." She was rubbing her arms to get the circulation going, staring in horror at the dead man's bloody face and neck. Fargo turned down the light and picked up the rope, tied it to one end of the bed and began paying it out the window.

"We're leaving, honey. I'll go down first. Don't slide down or you'll lose all the skin off your hands. Wrap your legs around the rope, and go hand over hand. Be quick but don't hurry." He looked out the window, glad they were at the back of the hotel. Luckily, the street was deserted, and the room was only one floor above the ground. In another moment he was going down the rope hand over hand.

On the ground he waited while the girl descended, waited a moment to listen but heard nothing from the room upstairs. Surely the shot must have been heard, if not the fight. But there was no time now to spend on speculation and he

58

started running down the deserted street, the girl following.

In moments they were at the livery.

"Knew what you was about, I reckon," the old hostler croaked as he led out the little buckskin.

Fargo handed him money.

The old man sucked his lower lip on his gums. "Knowed by the way you said you might need a hoss . . ." he croaked. Then, as Fargo stepped up into the saddle, "You ast where Hangtown was, mister."

"Where?"

"It's north and west, past Eagle Butte and Widow's Crossing." He croaked twice. "Exceptin', it ain't there no more. There ain't nothin' there, mister, exceptin' trouble."

There was no time for palaver. And they were out into the night, walking their horses quickly, not running them for fear of attracting attention, staying behind the livery and off main street. Pausing for a moment at the edge of town, Fargo listened, Sally sitting the buckskin beside him.

"Where are we heading?" she asked.

"Out of town." And he lifted the Ovaro into a fast canter.

Riding through the soft, starry night, he reflected on how something inside him had known he would need the extra pony. It was that extra sense he had always had since he was a shaver, that sense that had warned him and saved him time and again. He grinned to himself. By heaven, it seemed to be growing stronger.

Fargo threw a glance at the girl riding beside him. She was all right, he decided, even though ornery. His eyes felt over the high curves of her firm breasts. She was doing all right. She looked at him suddenly, an icy smile at her lips.

"It seems you do know your business, Fargo—the way you handled those men."

He grinned at her. "I've got other talents," he said. "Like handling women." And his grin broadened at her anger.

4

Buck had been a good choice. Not as fast as the Ovaro, yet a sturdy animal and sure. They hadn't much of a start, Fargo realized only too well. By now the room clerk would surely know that something was amiss, with the three not coming back downstairs.

The night was clear, with a crescent moon, and the Trailsman was careful to stay in the shadows. The air had cooled, and Fargo, shifting in his saddle, stole a look at the girl, noting that she was no stranger to a saddle horse, though, as he noted wryly to himself, she didn't know as much as she thought she did.

They had reached a shallow creek, and he drew rein.

"Are we stopping here?" Sally asked.

"Head downstream," he told her. "I'll follow. Stay right in the middle of the creek."

When they had gone a few yards, he told her to stop. "Now move your horse over and let him make just one print on the bank there, like you were still heading downstream."

He waited while she kneed the buckskin over to the bank.

"You want them to find that," she said.

"I'll give you an A-plus, ma'am." He had turned the Ovaro. "We'll head upstream now." At a small stand of box elders Fargo drew rein and ran his hand along an overhanging branch, bending it. Then he stepped out of the saddle and took the buckskin by his head stall and led him near the bank. He stopped and, lifting the horse's right hind leg, made a partial print in the mud.

He stood still, listening, his whole body keening to any sound of pursuit.

"So they'll think we went downstream and then turned around and came back up," the girl said. "Trying to throw them off. Then what? We fly?"

"That's right; we fly." He had reached into his saddlebag and come out with some wide strips of soft leather. Handing her some, he told her to wrap the buckskin's feet. "We'll make it on that bank there. There's stone, and we'll go slowly."

She was quick and efficient—like a good school marm, he was thinking. And in a little while they had both horses reshod with the makeshift moccasins. Twice the Trailsman stopped to listen but caught nothing. Finally he mounted up, signaling the girl to do the same, and they rode up and over the low bank. When they were some distance away, he dismounted again and returned, brushing out any grass that had been bent by the horses. Fortunately the moon had risen and he was able to see clearly.

He stopped to listen again; this time he heard them. It sounded like a good number, probably half a dozen at least. "We'll walk them to that stand of trees yonder," he said.

"Do you think it will work?" she asked, and he noted more than a trace of concern in her voice.

"That's a dumb question," he shot back.

"I don't think it's so dumb."

"Honey, either it works or it doesn't work. And thinking about it isn't going to make a damn bit of difference."

In silence they reached the stand of spruce and hemlock, and in a few minutes were through it and riding up a hard trail on the other side.

The trail suddenly lifted up, veered right and crossed over a low shoulder of rock. The moon was now covered by a cloud and the rock loomed black in the thin night. Soon the trail gave onto an open space, sloped down and then up again.

Now and again the Trailsman stopped to listen, his whole body open to the land, the sky, the wind that now and again stirred down from the high country.

"Are they still following?" Sally asked.

"Not anymore."

"Who were they?"

"I was going to ask you the same." They had dismounted at the edge of a small meadow.

Fargo let the Ovaro walk into a narrow stream of fairly deep water that rushed down from the rocks above them, and the girl followed suit with the buckskin.

"Let it come right up to his knees," he said. "We'll camp here, just back of the line of trees."

"I'm hungry," Sally said.

"There's beef jerky and a can of peaches in my war bag."

"Any coffee?"

"There is coffee, but we're not building a fire." She stared at him, her eyes sharp, tilting her head to one side, and he imagined that was how she confronted unruly children in the classroom.

"But I thought those men were no longer following us."

"They're not."

"So they can't smell the fire or the coffee," she said with triumph in her voice.

"True," he conceded, "but we don't have time." She started to object and he cut her off. "Now stop arguing so damn much—and tell me who those men were in the hotel."

She had seated herself with her back to the trunk of a cottonwood tree. "I don't know who they were."

"I had a notion one of them might have been from that bunch that hit the wagons, but I couldn't be sure."

"I had the thought that Kite Johnson sent them," she said. "He was pretty mad when I told him I wouldn't go through with the auction."

"What did you expect—a kiss?"

"I didn't expect such violence. He was beside himself, absolutely furious."

Fargo grunted. "So you decided to bring it all on top of me. Nice."

Her face fell. "I'm sorry. I couldn't think of any place else to hide." She bit her lower lip, her eyes searching his face. "I really am sorry, Fargo. I know I shouldn't have come to your room. But I had to hide; you see, Kite didn't actually want me for the auction so much as he—well, wanted *me*."

"People are always muddying things, aren't they?"

"It wasn't funny. I was scared. I don't mind admitting that."

"It's all right to be scared; it's not all right to be dumb."

She nodded, a low sigh coming from her. "He told me to think it over, and fast. I could go with him or I could pay for my passage. He wanted five hundred dollars."

"And so you took off."

"As soon as the auction started I took off. I'm sorry. I really made a mess of it."

"Sorry doesn't help," Fargo said. "Next time—if there is a next time—use your head." He watched the irritation jab into her shoulders and neck, become a tight line at her mouth.

"I couldn't have known Kite would go to those extremes, sending men after me and trying to beat you."

"Look," he said patiently. "You hired me to

65

help you. I'm trying to help. I'm trying to teach you some things so you can stay alive out here."

All at once she softened. "I—I—yes . . ."

"Better rest, but don't fall asleep. You'll be safe so long as you keep under cover of the trees. I'll be back before sunup."

"Back! Where are you going?"

"To Washing Springs," he said, handing her a pistol he took from his saddlebag.

"Washing Springs! But we just left there. I thought we were heading for Hangtown!"

"That's what those men following us are thinking. Keep that gun with you," he snapped. "You still talk too damned much!"

The town lay somnolent in the dead of night. There was no moon, for which he was thankful. The shabby buildings simply appeared like giant weeds on the great prairie as he rode in carefully from the northwest.

As he got closer lights showed from the half-dozen gaming and drinking establishments, but the rest of the town lay in total darkness.

The Trailsman rode slowly along the edge of the town, avoiding any light that would catch him and the Ovaro. As he passed in back of the Good Times a door suddenly burst open, a man reeled out, cursing, followed by the strains of "Chicken in the Bread Tray," the caller's soughing voice, the stomping of heavy feet and rocking laughter.

He had no trouble finding the little building—squat, narrow-shouldered and unpainted, in total darkness between the bank and the undertaker's parlor, a good distance from the revelry that now and again, here and there, burst suddenly into the night. Dismounting, he lay the Ovaro's reins loosely over the hitching rail at the side of the bank, so that if a swift departure was necessary, no time would be wasted. Silent as fog, he checked the street, moved swiftly to the back door of the marshal's office only a few yards from the small jail directly behind it. The danger was that Clyde Greenough might be inside his office taking a snooze.

In a moment he had jimmied open the locked door—a simple procedure—and had entered a sort of anteroom, leading into the office that gave onto Main Street. Suddenly he felt the cat against his leg and was grateful that he'd paid attention to the animal on his previous visit.

Reaching up, he took a wooden lucifer from his hatband and, with his back to the street window, lighted the stub of candle he had brought with him. It was chancy, no question, but even though he had memorized the contents of the room, he still had to see what he was after. Quickly he stepped up to the flyers hanging on the wall, removed them and carried them into the little room at the rear where the candlelight would not be so obvious to anyone who might happen to be in the street.

They went back a few years. There weren't a great many, but some were yellowed and torn. And there were two recent ones. Yet none with

the name Logan. Of course, names often
changed, especially in that line of work, he well
knew. But he found nothing that even appeared
to be a clue leading to John Logan. Returning to
the front room, he replaced the flyers, making
sure they appeared in the same disorder.

Shielding the candle, he stepped to the desk.
It was locked. There was a recent flyer lying on
top but the description had nothing to do with
what he knew of John Logan. Bending, he looked
into the wastebasket, but save for a two-week-old
newspaper, there was nothing. He took the
paper into the rear room and opened it. Something had been cut out of the center of the third
page—neatly with a blade. Returning to the
wastebasket he searched for the cutting but without any success. Quickly he undid the bandanna
that was around his neck, made a padding of it,
and wrapping it around the blade of the Arkansas
throwing knife, he forced open the lock of the
desk drawer. Some loose cartridges, a piece of
string, a blank piece of torn paper and two pencil
stubs. Nothing. He shut the drawer and now,
with a small piece of wire he took from his
pocket—and which he had brought just for this
purpose—he managed to work the lock shut. It
wasn't any too soon. In the next instant a sound
came from the street and he snuffed the candle,
stepping through the back room and out the
door. He regretted not having time to rid the
room of any smell of candle wax. As he shut the

back door of the little house he heard the key struggling in the lock at the front.

Quickly he moved the Ovaro so that he could mount instantly, then returned to the back window; he had a partial view through the rear room into the marshal's office. Two men had come in, Marshal Clyde Greenough and another he couldn't see. Then as the lamp was turned up Fargo saw the shadow of a derby hat on the far wall. They stood talking for a moment, then all at once Greenough came striding through the little building toward the back door. Fargo drew quickly away from the window as the door opened.

"Thought I smelled candle wax in there for a minute, Kite."

"Clyde, that was your upper lip." And the two men laughed together as they stood urinating into the night.

"That sonofabitch is probably all the way up to Indian territory by now," Kite said, his voice bold.

"And the girl."

"Damn bitch!" Kite Johnson buttoned his trousers furiously.

"Still the pickins was good," Greenough said. "Be happy with what you got and never mind the girl. As for that big sonofabitch, he's not the type to get previous with. You just better watch it. You seen what he did to the boys at the Buffalo Horn."

"I also seen what he done to Stacey and his bunch," snapped the little man.

"Business first, Kite. Rein those feelings about Stacey till we get our business done. We might need him and his boys."

"Need that sonofabitch!"

"Maybe let him and Boden knock each other over. You recollect how it was said Stacey told the law on Burl. And Kite, I need more protection fee. I kept Stacey and his boys hobbled during the auction, you'll of noticed. I'm sorry about what happened before."

Kite sniffed, good humor seeped reluctantly into his voice. "Good enough." Then, "You figure him and the girl is heading for Hangtown?"

"That's what he asked about. Had I ever heard of such a place."

"But his reasons. That's what we want to know."

"I got no idea. I asked him was he a bounty hunter. He said no."

"Could be lying."

"He could be on to something if he is looking for Hangtown."

"I know it."

"But we play it careful. We don't want the whole entire country knowing what's going on." Clyde Greenough spat and said, "He asked about a man name of Logan. You know that name?"

"Nope. I never. 'Course, man can change his name."

"That is a gut." The marshal of Washing

Springs spat again as he buttoned his fly, snorted and started back into the building.

Fargo waited a moment, then mounted the Ovaro and walked him quietly back along the edge of the town. On a hunch he circled around to the south side, stopping when he came to the livery barn. There was a light coming from the little room where the hostler stayed. But there was no sign of Hank, the old man.

Fargo dismounted, led the Ovaro to the side of the barn and then knocked on the door of the room. The room was empty. He was about to leave when he spied a small stack of newspapers by the jumbo stove.

Swiftly he went through them, checking the dates, but there was nothing corresponding to the paper in Clyde Greenough's office.

He had started across to the door that led to the barn proper when he heard the sound, a sort of thump, which at first he thought was a horse stomping. But then he heard it again. It was no horse. Drawing the Colt, he pulled open the door and stepped into the barn and away from the open doorway.

Then he saw Hank. The old man was lying alongside one of the stalls, trying to raise himself, and in so doing had thumped his boots against the wooden floor. His face was covered with blood; he was croaking, trying to speak.

Fargo helped him to his feet and walked him outside to the horse trough where he washed him down with a cloth. "Who did it?"

71

The old man didn't answer. He stood there weaving on his feet, his left eye swollen almost shut, his face skinned and maybe with a cracked rib or two; his head bent almost to his shoulder.

"You want to see the doc?"

"Nope."

"Why did they beat you?"

The old man croaked but didn't reply.

Only when he was sure Hank could handle himself, did Fargo decide to leave. Even then he waited, knowing the risk he was taking with Greenough and Kite about. But old Hank was coming round.

"I'll make it."

"It was on account of you renting the buckskin, wasn't it?"

The old man looked at him, his jaws clamped shut, and said nothing. But Fargo knew he had struck something.

As he walked Hank back to his stable room he spotted the newspaper in the sagging overalls pocket. Then, easing the old man down into his chair, he slipped the newspaper out of his pocket.

"Thank ye," followed by a croak.

"You all right?"

"I'll make it." And he croaked twice. "Too bad I ain't twenty years younger, I'd clean the sonsofbitches' clock right now."

"Right, young feller. But I'm twenty years younger," Fargo said grimly as he walked to the Ovaro and took a bottle of whiskey out of his saddlebag. "You going to tell me who?" He had found a glass and was filling it with whiskey.

The old man's eyes were fixed eagerly on the amber fluid. "Nope."

Fargo put the glass on the table.

"You're a good man, Hank." And he slipped the bottle back into the saddlebag and mounted the horse.

It was still dark when he rode up and out of a low coulee and the little clearing lay below him. It would be dawn soon, but there'd be time for coffee.

The girl was sitting up, with her back against a large rock, the gun in her hand.

"It's me," he said softly. "Fargo." And she jumped. He was almost beside her when he spoke.

"My God, you're so quiet."

"You'll never last long like that."

"But you never made a sound."

"You could've smelled the horse and leather," he said.

"What happened in town? Did you find what you were looking for?"

"I dunno." And then he said, "Anything happen out here while I was gone?"

"Nothing."

"Get some sleep."

"You told me not to."

"You get some sleep now," he said. "An hour."

After she had rolled into her blanket, he took a

look around the campsite. Everything appeared in order, and presently he lay down on his bedroll, the Colt by his hand, and closed his eyes. He lay there thinking of the news item he had read on page 3 of the *Gebo Gazette*. It was short, simply stating that Burl Boden, the famous outlaw and former scourge of Tensleep County, had served his term of imprisonment in Laramie penitentiary and was being released. Boden, known as one of the West's most notorious outlaws, had been marshal of Washing Springs, Wyoming Territory, when it had been a thriving mining community while at the same time he ran an outlaw operation that robbed stages, banks and individuals with marked success for a number of years. When the mines ran out, Boden was captured in a holdup at Medicine Rock, Montana, and returned to Wyoming. In his heyday Burl Boden and his gang had headquartered at an almost impregnable "Robbers' Roost" in the Bear Paw Mountains.

In the morning Fargo awakened to the sweet smell of morning rain. It was falling softly, more a drizzle than actual drops. And then suddenly the sun appeared through the mist that covered the land, and the gray wrapping of the dawn loosened and blue skies framed the meadows, the creeks, the great rising of the Bear Paw Mountains.

Fargo sat up, watching the beaded rain glistening on the blades of grass, the steam rising from the flanks of the dampened horses.

The girl was still asleep as he dressed quickly. With his field glasses he studied carefully every ravine, canyon, gulch, each cluster of pine caught on the face of a cliff lining the great valley beyond the creek.

Could someone have trailed them this far, this high?

Behind him he heard the girl stir in her blanket.

"It's like wine." Her words weren't for him, he realized, but spoken to the land and sky, and to herself. "It's truly beautiful."

"We'll have coffee," he said, turning, and his glance caught her bare thighs as she pulled on her trousers. A joyous tingle raced through him. Quickly she threw the blanket over herself, her face darkening.

"Do you have to continually stare at me when I'm getting dressed."

"You said the view was beautiful and I'm agreeing," he answered mildly. "When are you going to stop being such a prude?"

"Never!"

He ignored her while he built a fire and put the coffee on, then he drew two hard sourdough biscuits from his pocket. "Best to soak these jaw-breakers in the coffee," he said. "They're a bit stale."

She accepted the hard biscuit in silence, still smarting under their earlier exchange. Then he drew out some wild plums and raspberries that he'd picked along the trail.

They ate in silence and drank the coffee. "Do you remember anything in your father's letter that might have had more to say about Hangtown?"

She considered, then shook her head. "No. I can't say I do. He just said he was writing from a place called Hangtown. Something like that. I don't remember his exact words."

"Does the name Boden mean anything to you?"

"No. Why do you ask?"

"Just a name I heard," he said.

He rose and saddled the Ovaro. Then he watched her saddling the buckskin, saw the animal swell his belly when she cinched up. But he said nothing, watching as she put her foot in the stirrup, started up into the saddle and landed on the ground on her back. The loosely cinched saddle was twisted halfway down the buckskin's side.

"Damn!"

"You've got to watch him when he swells his belly like that," Fargo said calmly.

"Why didn't you warn me, damn you!"

"Best way to learn, making mistakes," he said. "Besides, you never listen to me."

She stood and began resaddling the horse while Fargo watched, admiring her tight, curving rump as she lifted the heavy stock saddle onto the horse.

When she had mounted the buckskin, he began erasing any trace of their having been in the little clearing.

"I thought you said they had lost our trail," she remarked. "So why are you going through all of that?"

"We're not very far from Indian country," he said. "I'd like to keep my hair on."

She seemed to think a moment. "You mean you left me alone up here where there was the chance of Indians coming?"

He nodded. "But I wasn't worried."

"*You* weren't worried!"

"Figured anything happened, you could talk them out of it."

He walked again to the edge of the clearing and with the glasses once more studied the long, wide country to see if any changes had taken place. Below, the river ran like a silver ribbon through cottonwoods, drawing a line right through the center of the great valley. Far across the valley the only things moving were some small black spots on a distant bench of land. He figured them to be a grazing herd of horses. And beyond? Beyond, the land rose again into the Bear Paws, into Shoshone country. But where was Hangtown?

Now they rode carefully through a sloping patch of dark brush followed by a field of green juniper. For a short distance a brilliant black-and-yellow butterfly teased around him. Fallen, petrified trees lay scattered on all sides. And the sweet smell of the early morning rain was still there.

Silently they rode down, down. The near slopes of the valley rose toward them as the cliffs and peaks lifted higher behind them. And at last they came to the stubby, tawny-colored plain below.

Stopping, he picked more wild plums and raspberries, which they ate hungrily.

At noontime he reined the pinto and they let the horses drink at a shallow creek while Fargo and the girl dismounted and lay belly down, drinking the cool, restorative water.

He rose, squinting at the noontime sun.

"Is Hangtown far?" She stood looking up at him, her shirt wet from the creek and taut over her pushing, vibrant breasts. He watched the nipples harden involuntarily as he looked at them.

"I don't know if Hangtown is far," he said in answer to her question. "But we'd better get started if we're ever going to get there."

He stepped into the saddle, swinging his leg over the high cantle as Sally mounted the buckskin and the pair set off across the creek, their horses' hooves striking on the stones.

An hour later he reined the Ovaro.

"What is it?" Sally Logan asked.

He was listening.

"We're being followed."

5

He knew it had to be chance that someone had cut their trail, for he'd taken pains to cover their tracks well. Kite Johnson? Greenough? Or was it the Shoshone? An Indian could be actively tracking them, he knew. Or someone highly skilled in the craft of tracking. Or it could be someone who was simply riding in the general direction of Hangtown anyway.

And now as he crouched waiting by the two big slabs of rock at the bend in the trail where it wound up and back on itself, he heard the ring of a horseshoe on stone. That was no Indian riding a shod pony. It could only be a white man.

He waited, letting the breath leave his body easily, careful not to suck in air and so become tight. He felt loose. He was aware of the girl a few feet behind him, holding the horses. He had told her to keep her hand over the buckskin's muzzle so he wouldn't whiffle. He wasn't concerned about the Ovaro; he had trained him.

His hold on the Sharps was loose, while his

lake-blue eyes focused through the opening between the two big rocks and onto the trail below. Whoever was coming would have to appear through the stand of petrified trees and stumps into the clear lines of the Trailsman's sight.

Sally moved closer to him and he felt the change of atmosphere.

"How many?" she whispered.

He held up two fingers.

"Are they close?"

Without turning his head, he nodded, smelling her yet refusing to allow thoughts of her to intrude. He listened, catching the spaces in between the sounds that came from the land around him, the little echoes that were at the edge of the day, the shadow sounds. Whoever was coming up the trail was making little attempt to be quiet now.

And then suddenly he heard the croak, and at that same moment Hank the hostler rode out of the trees and into Fargo's sights. But Fargo's surprise was doubled when he saw the second rider. He didn't need to hear the sharp intake of Sally's breath to tell him it was Frannie. She was riding a little blue roan he had spotted in the livery back at Washing Springs. There was a large black-and-blue welt on the side of her face.

"Hold it!" he called, the words sharp.

Without a second's hesitation the old hostler yanked back on the sorrel mare he was riding, the roan, directly behind, almost colliding into her rump.

They were camped now in the presence of an extraordinary sunset, the light almost painful as it stretched across the wide valley and up the foothills into the willows and box elders along the bank of the flashing stream.

"So how is married life?" Fargo asked wryly as he took in Frannie's battered face. And he remembered how he had asked her that same question two days before in Washing Springs when they met in the street.

Frannie looked appealingly toward Sally, returned her eyes to Fargo. "Beautiful!" She took a deep breath, her breasts swelling superbly as they pushed aside the opening of her jacket. "I must have been crazy to consider such a thing." And she turned her head to show him more clearly the large welt on the side of her face.

"Frannie . . ." Sally started to reach out her hand in sympathy, stopped, biting her lip. Then, shaking her head in wonder, "Why—why?"

"Drunk." The tears welled in Frannie's green eyes, but she held them, her bruised lips trembling. "You should see some other parts of my body."

"Where is he now?" Fargo asked.

She shrugged, and he could see it was painful for her to do so. Yet she was able to smile at herself. "Probably sleeping it off. Him and Stacey."

"Stacey!"

"Miller and Stacey are buddies."

"My God!" Sally was staring in awe at her friend. "Did they both beat you?"

"You don't know what you missed, Sal," Frannie said ruefully. "You know, Kite Johnson is after you." She turned to Fargo. "I heard he sent the men who broke into your hotel room."

Fargo had been squatting by the small fire, holding his cup of coffee loosely in his hands. He squinted toward Hank, who had hardly spoken since they'd met on the trail, then turned back to Frannie. "So you ran off, rented the horse from Hank here . . ." He looked again at the hostler who still showed bruises on his face, still sat with his head bent halfway to his shoulder. "You're a pair for sore eyes, the two of you," he said sardonically. "Doesn't anyone shoot people anymore? They just beat 'em to death?"

To which old Hank croaked, a tight smile slashing across his face as he twisted his body to look at Fargo. "Saving on ammunition, wouldn't you say?" He sniffed, croaked again. "When she told me she was looking for you, I figured to come and join you too, if you'd have me. You said Hangtown." The voice rasped; Hank's Adam's apple pumped in his stringy throat. "I can't take another beating. I'd like to throw in with you for a spell anyways. If you'd have me," he repeated.

Fargo had kept his eyes on the old man while he spoke, watching the effort it cost him to ask—

not just the physical effort. And yet there was not a trace of self-pity or begging.

He nodded. "Good enough, old-timer."

Nor was there self-pity in the girl. By God, he liked her spirit. Beaten, thwarted in her effort to start a new life, she'd nearly gone from the fire right into the deep six, yet she was smiling. The two of them revealed an inner dignity that touched him.

Now, looking at her long, shapely body in the tight calico skirt with the short jacket unable to close over her proud, prominent breasts, he decided she looked radiant. Those high, bouncy breasts were like twin flags proclaiming her.

"We'll breathe the horses a bit longer," he said. "And ourselves." He nodded to Sally. "Take her upstream a bit. Water's good for the body, and I've got arnica you can put on her."

Sally jumped to her feet. "Come on, Fran. Let me take a look at those bruises."

Fargo suppressed a grin. It was the school marm speaking, even though she was being kind. That stiffness was clearly in her body as well, and yet . . . His eyes followed her tight buttocks in smooth black pants as she walked away. It wasn't only her body holding back, he decided. There was definitely something else. At the same time, in spite of the rigidity, she revealed a young girl's awkward grace.

When they had disappeared into the trees along the stream bank, he turned to the old hostler. "There's whiskey."

A grin flicked into the lined face. "Knowed I come to the right place," the old man said, and croaked. "Though it'll be one. Got to keep sharp. Like the girl said, Kite'll be after us and more'n likely Greenough and maybe more with him. You know they're partners."

Fargo nodded, at the same time appreciating the caution and resolve of the hostler.

"We took some time covering tracks down below on the other side of the river."

Fargo studied the old man, who was having trouble with his breathing after taking a sizable swallow of whiskey. "How far are we from Hangtown, Hank?"

The old man licked his lips, ran the back of his wrist across his mouth. "Well, it ain't the distance, it's more the what you got to get through to get there."

"Like what, for instance?"

"Like maybe the Shoshone."

"I didn't know it was tribal land."

"Didn't used to be, but since it got so, people moved away. Had to."

"Is that why people I asked said they didn't know where it was?"

"Could be. Or it could be they was fearing something."

"Like what?"

"Like Burl Boden maybe coming back, and maybe some others who are interested in his coming back. Like Dutch Stacey and some others have suddenly showed up again. People don't want to mess with it." He wheezed then, croaked, gasped like a teakettle coming to the boil, and Fargo realized that like any old-timer he loved to talk, yet because of his handicap hadn't much opportunity.

"How come they're so concerned about Boden?"

The old man's mouth worked as though he was trying to locate a piece of food or maybe chewing tobacco. "Likely on account Burl's supposed to of hid money someplace, and could be the boys figure some of it is theirs." He looked speculatively at Fargo. "How come you are concerned—like about Hangtown?"

"I am looking for a man named John Logan."

"Don't know him."

"It's Sally's father."

"Thought you was hunting Burl Boden, being as you're looking for Hangtown." Hank was staring at him with his eyes very wide.

"Could be I am," Fargo said slowly, and his forehead wrinkled thoughtfully as he lifted his head and looked up at the sky. "Maybe Boden could give me news on John Logan." He looked at the old hostler again. The bent head wagged and a croak came from the wrinkled throat.

"They call you the Trailsman."

"That's right."

"You figger to find this Logan feller?"

"That's what I've been hired to do."

Something like a chuckle filled Hank's throat, his face and on down through his shoulders and

85

chest. This turned into a coughing fit, followed by hawking and spitting.

Fargo waited while the old man subsided into wheezing and finally a couple of croaks.

"Jesus, Trailsman." And his eyes seemed almost on fire with excitement. "Jesus, there's gonna be more people out there looking for Burl Boden's cache than a dog can piss at!"

"A sizable cache?"

"You may be lookin' for her old man, Fargo—I got no doubt—but I'll bet the last hair on my ass Burl Boden is headin' right back here to Hangtown for the same reason everybody else is."

"For his cache."

"What him and his gang took from all them stages and banks." The old man smacked his lips, his eyes gleaming. "Shit, must be thousands!"

Shortly after dark the storm hit them with rolling thunder and streaks of lightning flashing across the black sky. Its suddenness was unnerving, and Fargo felt the fear coming from the two women as he settled them under an overhang of rock near some box elders and ash at the bottom of a cliff.

No one except Fargo had bedding, but the horse blankets served. And he had built a fire. Shortly, they had warmed and dried and were relaxed. He had shot two jackrabbits in the afternoon and these he now cooked. And Hank had collected some plums and berries along the way. They were all ravenous, and the meal, washed down with good hot coffee, put everyone in good spirits.

When the meal was finished and the women were settled and Hank had bedded down in another protected opening, Fargo ran through the driving rain to where he had spread his bedroll several yards away under a similar overhang of rock. It was a good spot, dry, and he had a good view if anyone approached.

He sat on his bedroll now, watching the storm; the lightning stabbed through the stygian sky, now and again illuminating the soaking horses huddled beneath the trees. It was cold, but he didn't build a second fire; one fire was enough of a risk.

Then—it must have been around midnight— the storm stopped suddenly. Silence stretched over the land, save for the wet sound of water dripping through the trees as it fell to the shining ground.

Fargo had just lain down when he heard her running lightly over the ground. And he knew he had been expecting her.

Frannie was out of breath as he opened his bed for her.

"Please, Fargo," she gasped. "Help me. Help me wash it all away."

She had only underpants on beneath her long nightdress and he slid his hand inside, under her firm, thrusting buttocks, bringing his long finger through her legs to tantalize the wet lips.

"Aaaaah . . . aah . . . ah . . ." and her legs

spread wide for him as his finger thrust deeper, and her mouth sucked into his. Now she reached up and took his head and pulled him down to her big mounds, glistening with perspiration, pushing one now the other into his face, his mouth, while his tongue tickled the hard, bursting nipples to the ecstatic rhythm of her begging and moaning.

"Christ, Fargo . . . oh my God . . . dear Jesus . . . Fargo!" She reached down, tore off her underpants and grabbed his rigid maleness, pumping it, her fist sliding on its wetness. And then her lips were on it as she bent and licked, still moaning, panting, now taking the whole of the big stick deep in her mouth, almost gagging as he plunged it in and she began to suck with a slow stroke, then increasing the tempo, and returning with a slow rhythm, while his finger played deep inside the marvelous bush between her pumping legs.

"Give it to me, Fargo . . . please God, give it!" She rolled onto her back, grabbing his cock in her fist and guiding it to her begging orifice, as her buttocks still pumped wildly.

He was on his hands and knees looking down at her, resisting her demand for the ultimate.

"Jesus, Fargo . . . let me have it! Don't torture me. Oh God, don't stop . . . don't . . . don't stop! Aieeeeee!"

And he plunged his huge member deep and hard into her, twisted and rotated his hips while she cried out again, screamed, digging her fingers like a tigress into his pushing buttocks.

Slowly now he drew his weapon out right to the tip, until she grabbed him, wrapping her legs around his back, scissoring him with her untamable passion. Finally, he drove it into her, shoving it like a ramrod right up as high as it would go, hitting bottom as she gasped, cried, fought it and won it—pumping, squirming and finally subsiding into silence after the explosion. . . .

Following the storm they were up early and in the spectacular dawn rode north and west. At noon they were at the outside edge of the reservation that had been assigned to Chief Red Wolf and his large band. Fargo called a halt to rest and water the horses by a stream of crystal-clear water that came spilling down a huge face of rock.

"We could get into that nice cold water," he suggested.

"I for one could stand a change of clothing," Frannie announced.

And Sally echoed with, "I want a bath."

Fargo stepped down from the big pinto and stood looking up at the two women, who were still on their horses. "Ladies, the water is free, and the drying sun is free. And—uh—your humble guide is free."

Frannie laughed, but Sally muttered coldly, "Humble indeed!" as she dismounted from the buckskin and walked off with Frannie to another part of the stream.

Without waiting till they were out of sight, Fargo pulled off his clothes and plunged into the icy water.

Hank, unable to match his speed, struggled out of his shirt and trousers, unlaced his boots and shuffled reluctantly into the water, croaking gently, softly splashing himself and cursing.

Afterward they lay on the bank, warming themselves in the sun, idly listening to the two women a short distance away and out of sight. Pretty soon a snore broke from the old hostler.

Lying on his back, Fargo smiled up at the sky. Presently his thoughts turned to John Logan. Had he been in Boden's gang? It sounded as though he had. Maybe he actually was Boden? Easy enough to change a name.

And where did Clyde Greenough fit into the picture? The marshal had cut out the clipping on Boden from the newspaper, but was it only as part of his job? Were the marshal and Kite Johnson engaged in more than the women's auctions? He was sure that Greenough, at any rate, was up to something in connection with Boden. There had been that moment in his office when he'd asked whether John Logan carried any identifying marks.

Under the warmth of the sun Fargo's thoughts skipped to the pleasures of Frannie and the tantalizing inaccessibility of Sally Logan. The damned girl had almost bitten him when he'd offered her coffee earlier that morning. It had become instantly clear what was bothering her, however.

"Some people make enough noise not sleeping—as they ought to be doing—to deafen a cavalry charge," she had snapped at him, her eyes flashing.

To which he had replied, "Well, honey, some people like to listen to grown-ups, and then some like to do like the grown-ups."

"I just hope that tonight the rest of us can get some sleep!"

"Aw come on, Sal." Frannie had walked over and slipped her arm around her friend's waist. "Sometimes people have nightmares at night."

"Nightmares, my foot! I'm not mad at you, mind you. But—at this—*person*, who ought to know better!"

"I have a question," Fargo said, pushing his Stetson hat onto the back of his head. "Why is it that school marms always look so pretty when they're mad?"

She stood facing him, her hands on her hips. She was wearing tight tan trousers and a lemon-colored blouse that fully revealed her figure. Pleasured though he had been by Frannie, Fargo still felt an insatiable hunger mounting in him for the snooty young lady standing there with her full red lips parted, a delightful lock of dark brown hair falling almost into her hazel eyes.

"Sal, come on," Frannie urged. "It isn't worth all that sweat."

"I'm sorry. I'm sorry, Frannie." The words were spoken out of barely controlled anger. Now she forced herself to be calm as she said, "I know you've been through a lot, and I'm sorry I got upset. It's just that—that man is so damned conceited. . . ." Her words had faded as they walked away.

Yet when he saw her again, she had returned to her usual civil—though bordering on aloof—manner.

They had been riding across a meadow when she'd asked him why they were traveling so slowly. "Don't you think we could go a little faster?"

"If we want to get there at all, it's best to take the time," he said, accepting her effort at reconciliation, although he was well aware of her impatience. "You've waited this long," he continued. "Why spoil it now?"

"How spoil it? What's to spoil in trying to move along at a faster pace?"

"For one thing we'll be riding through someone else's country and we don't want to attract attention; and we also want to be respectful, which comes to much the same."

"Someone else's land? What do you mean?"

"Up yonder is the start of the reservation. That's Indian land."

"Oh." She flushed slightly. And he was surprised as an expression came into her face that he'd not seen before. "May I ask you a question, Mr. Fargo?"

"Go ahead."

"It's personal, but anyway . . . Are you Indian or part Indian?"

"Why do you ask that?"

"I admire the proficiency you reveal in your actions, as I have already told you, and—uh—even in your thinking. I mean about tracking and survival in the wilds," she added stiffly. "I don't approve of the way the Indians are being treated, by the way."

He studied her a moment, weighing her for sincerity. "I'll tell you something, Miss Logan. And it isn't fancy. It's something an old Cherokee told me a long time ago. He said, 'Being Indian isn't a thing of the blood, it's a way of life.'"

"I see." And once again her expression surprised him. For he was sure she was embarrassed.

"Do you think if I was Indian, that would explain me better?" he speared at her.

She had recovered and was back in her usual role. "No," she answered coolly. "Not at all. I believe you'd be just as conceited and rude no matter what you were!" And with a devastatingly sweet smile she turned away. While he, with a big grin on his face, kicked the Ovaro into a fast trot.

It was about halfway through the forenoon when they sat their horses in the little copse of elm and willow, looking down at the man with his face buried in the mud near the spring.

A short, muffled gasp escaped Frannie, while Sally, with the suggestion of a tremor in her voice, asked, "Is he . . . dead?"

Fargo had already stepped out of his saddle as Hank croaked out something nobody heard.

"He's dead," the Trailsman said, squatting next to the half-naked body of the Indian. "Shot in the back." He tilted back his big hat, sniffed the air for gunpowder or the bear grease favored by Indians. "Awhile back, I'd say. At least, it smells clear around here."

"Shosh—Shosh—hone?" croaked Hank.

"He was." Fargo addressed himself to the ground near the dead man, his eyes searching everywhere. He had not touched the body, but now, having studied the terrain, he put his hand on the dead man's bare back. "Give me a hand, Hank. I want to turn him, but easy like."

When the old man had dismounted, together they carefully turned the body onto its back. A young, handsome warrior was staring up at them. Fargo studied the face for a minute, thinking, wondering at a young man being shot in the back on Indian land. Rising, he walked a few steps away and hunkered down by a rotted log. "Two horses. One iron-shod, the other an Indian pony." His eyes moved. "They waited here awhile; the men must've been talking, over there."

"How can you tell that?" Sally asked. "How do you know those men were talking there, and the horses waited for them?"

94

He looked up at her, his thumb and forefinger on his chin as he leaned his elbows on his knees. "Prints over there. They were sitting. The horses here, you can tell by those droppings in the two piles. Shows they weren't being ridden or the droppings would be spread out."

Hank was staring at him, scratching his head, twisting his shoulders to the side whenever he wanted to see better.

"Man had range boots," Fargo went on, reading sign. He looked up quickly at the two women, who had started to dismount. "Stay on your horses. There are enough tracks already."

"Does it mean trouble, Fargo?" Frannie's green eyes were wide with concern.

"Trouble would be a mild word, I'd say." His attention bent to the ground again. "So they were talking. Then they mounted up. Or—no, one of them mounted, the Shoshone. And he started off, leading the shod horse. Why?" He looked up at the two women and Hank. "Why would an Indian, after meeting a white man and talking with him on foot, mount up and ride off with the white man's horse?"

"Could it be the Indian bought the horse?" Sally asked.

"More than likely they were gambling and he won it," Fargo replied. "It's not uncommon, and they bet everything, the Indians—even horse and gun and even a woman, if they happen to have one." He paused. "He would have won the white man's gun, but he was shot off his horse."

He nodded toward the body. "That means the man afoot had a hideout. So he could be a gambler, maybe owlhooter."

"But Fargo, how can you say he got shot off his horse?" Frannie wanted to know.

He looked at Sally. "Schoolteachers get paid for answering questions, don't they?" he said amiably, and she smiled tightly. But before she could answer he said, "He's not a big man, not heavy, but he made an impression in the mud there, so he had to have fallen from a certain height." He ran his forefinger along his jaw, thinking. Then he said, "We've been here longer than I want. Let's get him hidden, Hank. Give us a little time before they find him."

When they had hidden the body in some bushes well away from the trail, Fargo told the three of them to ride on ahead, while he began erasing the tracks they had made. In a short while he mounted the Ovaro and followed Hank and the two women along the trail, leaving the body of the young Shoshone warrior to the wind, the sky and the buzzards. He knew it would not be very long before Red Wolf's people found him.

He had considered taking the body with them to hide it further on, but it would have slowed them considerably. Pursuit was inevitable, no matter how hard he attempted to cover their trail. The best thing was to get moving fast and stay light.

He said as much to old Hank, who sniffed and seemed to gargle, and who now all at once came to life. He even appeared to straighten a little, his eyes brightened, and he opened and closed his hand as though it was a strange thing.

Fargo grinned; the old warrior wasn't done for yet. There was, in fact, something about the old man that hadn't yet been revealed. He knew something; of that Fargo was sure.

"We'll cut for Hangtown direct as we can," he told Hank. "You know the trail. The quicker we get there the better."

Hank twisted his body in his saddle so that he could look at Fargo. "See that rock jutting out yonder?" He nodded toward the far mountain, the rimrocks cut clear against the spectacular sky.

"That far, is it?"

"Not all that far. Drop your eye down from that rimrock there and there's another place—Franc's Peak. That's Hangtown. Or was. It ain't called anything anymore."

"Rough going, I take it."

"It is all hardpan, solid rock and cussin'. Nothing grows there excepting dead men."

"Sounds inviting."

"That's how Burl Boden put it."

"Do you figure he'll maybe be there already, Hank?"

"With a man like Boden, anything is likely."

Fargo pondered it for a moment. "What about

97

feed for their horses? They'd need that in such a place."

"There is a meadow. Surprise you it would. You don't see it till you're about in it. It's a good place and like I say, well hid."

"Except from the Shoshone."

Old Hank twisted halfway out of his saddle to spit clear. Fargo had already noted how he tried to keep neat. "It was a damn fool thing to do, killing that Indian. Could start a whole war."

"Whoever did it could be up ahead of us. Could be someone after that cache."

Now the trail broke out of the trees and into open land. Rounding a low cutbank, Fargo watched a flock of geese suddenly sweep the brilliant sky as the hot sun burst down upon them. They rode quickly, the soft grass whispering against the swift hooves of their horses.

Presently they began moving to the higher country again, the long foothills sloping up to the timber. Here, they began picking their way single file along the narrow, winding trail, through pine, fir and hemlock.

The newspaper piece had called Hangtown a robbers' roost and Hank confirmed it. "The boys had it well forted," he told Fargo, croaking a little less now, it seemed, as he unbent more, finding someone to listen to him.

"You mean the gang. Boden's gang."

"Them and some others used the place. But mostly Burl and his boys."

Once again they rested the horses, high up now, near the rimrocks. Yet there was feed. There was bunch grass and they let the horses chomp on it. The Ovaro was cropping easily, his bit jangling in the thin air, while Hank's sorrel mare followed suit, kicking now and again at flies or turning her head suddenly to snap at her rump, her tail swishing, and sometimes shaking flies from her head and mane. It was noon and the day hummed with the heat and the crackling grass.

The hostler was looking at Fargo out of his bright eyes, his head bent, but it still seemed to Fargo that it was less bent than before. Yet Hank had difficulty. Fargo looked at the taut tendon on the exposed side of his leathery neck. He wondered if it hurt.

Suddenly the old man spoke. "You been wondering how come I know so much about Hangtown."

"Figured you'd tell me you were one of the gang—when you were ready," Fargo said as his weight shifted on the Ovaro, who was biting at the flies buzzing into his belly and crotch.

"I wasn't like a regular member. I didn't ride with the boys. I did their blacksmithing mostly. Chores. Like that." He paused. "Fact is, I got my neck busted out there at Hangtown, and my foot. The boys had been drinking. Myself included. And Stacey, he started jabbing at me, making fun and getting kind of close to the knuckle. He was always making a dig at somebody."

"Stacey again."

"The same gent. We liked hijinxing, but Stacey, he'd go too far. This time he set off a firecracker right under my horse, just as I set my foot in the stirrup. Well, Jesus! That little horse—he was a buckskin like hers, there—" And he nodded toward Sally, whose horse was cropping bunch grass only a few yards away. "He spun, he did, crow-hopped; and like I wasn't even in the saddle, but I got up on him; then by God he sunfished and cracked me right in the balls, and I went ass over teakettle, and he come down on my neck with his hoof." He paused, croaking and snorting and trying to get more air. But he was determined to tell it all. "And by jingo, that wasn't the whole of it neither; I got up mad as hell, not even feeling any pain, and I went for that sonofabitch Stacey, only I didn't look and I stepped right smack dab in a pile of real wet horse manure and skidded, and that pulled the shit out of my neck, especially when I landed on it. I felt like the goddamn mountain had fell on me. Pulled it all out of line, and the damn doc over to Gebo never could fix it. Been like this ever since, with the rheum in it to boot. Then my horse stepped on my foot."

"And Stacey?" Fargo asked.

"I told Stacey, I said; 'I am making you a promise, you sonofabitch.' I mean I told him right then when I was lying in that pile of horse shit. I said, 'I am making you a promise; I get myself repaired, I'll be coming for you, and I will break your fucking head open!' "

After a moment Fargo said, "Man makes a promise like that, he's got to keep it, and the other man knows that."

"That's what I know." He was gasping from the effort of so much talk and emotion. His eyes were squinting in the sharp light. "Only I never did get myself repaired. And I owe the sonofabitch for this here too," he added, touching his face.

"Then it was Stacey beat you."

"On account of I rented you that buckskin. He found out you were with that gal he wanted, see."

They fell silent, and after a few moments Fargo kneed the big pinto back onto the trail; the others followed. As they rode through a clearing he watched the sunlight touching the blades of grass, and through a gap in the trees his eyes found the snowy peaks of the far, high mountains.

The horses were well rested and as they rode deeper into the afternoon Fargo began putting it together. So Stacey had been in the Boden gang too. And maybe the others who had been at the wagons and in the hotel room. And maybe John Logan? In any event, Stacey would be after the cache, and very likely Greenough and Kite Johnson as well. And Logan—or was he really Boden? Boden could even be there already, waiting for them.

He asked Hank more about Boden.

"Burl? He run everything; even though he had lieutenants, there was no mistake he was the big candy. See, he was the marshal and he also run the outlaws. Get it?" A chuckle fell through Hank's lips. "He was marshal of Washing Springs, Gebo, Horse Crossing, a whole big piece. What you call a sheriff actually. He knew everything going on. Had spies who told him all about shipments—stock and the mines both, the stage runs."

"What kind of man was he?"

"Tough. Tough as whang leather. Smart as a whip. Faster'n a snake's tongue when it came to weapons. And accurate! I seen him stick a row of wooden lucifers on a corral rail and then step off thirty paces. There was six in the row of them matches, and Burl he lighted three of them with his big Navy Colt. I am saying at thirty feet!"

The old man fell from wheezing to coughing, and for a moment it got so bad Fargo had to hand him the bottle.

"Man's best friend, that fluid." He gasped into total silence finally and they rode, still in silence, toward Hangtown.

They were very close to their destination the night Frannie visited him again. She came to him almost before the others were asleep.

"I can't help it, Fargo. I'm going crazy rubbing against that hot saddle all day long, thinking about it, feeling it. It's torture."

"I told you it could become a habit," he said as he drew her down beside him.

"Thank God for that!"

"What about your friend?" he said.

"Sal? Don't mind her. I had a good talk with her. She's lonely, she's jealous and—she's a virgin."

"A virgin!"

"And let's keep her that way. She'll be all right." She slipped her bare arms around his neck. "Let me handle your needs, Mr. Fargo."

"Think you're able to?"

"I take that as a challenge and an offer."

"Just take it," he whispered in her ear.

She drew back, a smile teasing her lips, and rising up on her elbow, with her other hand she began to touch his chest, moving her fingers slowly down over the flat hardness of his abdomen.

"All day . . . all day, Fargo, I couldn't stop thinking about it. . . ."

He reached over and cupped a pillowy breast, circled his finger around the high, pink, eager nipple. Her breath pulled into her as she came closer to him, dropping down to lie half on top of him, pressing her breasts onto his hard-muscled chest. He felt her hand on his abdomen again, pulling away his shorts, and then her fist closed on his pulsating maleness.

"Ah, God . . ." she breathed, rolled onto her back, her legs spreading as she pulled him on top of her. "Fargo, please, give it, please God,

103

Fargo, God almighty . . . I beg you, Fargo, Far
. . . GO!"

He held back as he felt her beginning to
quiver.

"Oh God no, Fargo. Come to me, come to
me!"

But he insisted, moving in and out with
maddening slowness, from side to side, then
circling.

"Yes . . . oh, oh my God, yes, yes, yes . . ."
she breathed, gathering herself slowly, letting it
build, savoring the impossible sweetness of it.
Now the trembling ecstasy grew faster to unleash
itself in her driving loins as their two rhythms
became one, while her hands pulled him to her
writhing, thrusting and finally racing buttocks as
together they found the unique pulsation to
which they could both surrender, and it was no
longer bodies demanding, craving, pulsing, but
desire driving to the ultimate moment of dissolu-
tion and peace.

In the morning he was pleased to find that
Sally had her disapproval under control and was
even pleasant to him. She always managed to
look fresh, and he admired that. It wasn't easy for
either of the women to keep their spirits up on a
tough trail. But they were both spirited, none-
theless.

And then they rode down a long winding draw,
turned north again around a cutbank and began
to go up, the trail by now extremely narrow. Sud-

denly as they came around a bend they faced a broken, weatherbeaten board nailed to a tree stump. It was askew, one nail having rusted away.

WELCOME TO HANGTOWN

PEOPLE	2̶5̶	2̶3̶	2̶2̶	1̶8̶	13
DOGS	10				
CATS	1̶2̶	1̶1̶	10		
LAWMEN	0				

"Look," Fargo said, and they raised their eyes from the sign on the tree stump to where he was looking.

From the big branch of a cottonwood tree that spread high above the signboard, three ropes dangled. They were well along to rotting completely away, but there was no mistaking their purpose, each displaying enough of an aged hangman's knot for illustration.

Looking farther where Fargo now pointed, they saw something through the leaves and branches of a second cottonwood. And as the wind stirred the leaves that were blocking the view they all saw the body swinging slowly.

"My God . . ." Sally's words were barely audible. "It's someone . . ."

Fargo had ridden close to the corpse. It must have been a couple of days old; it was a white man. The body was riddled with arrows.

"Shoshone," Fargo said.

"Indians using white man's justice," muttered

Hank. "The sonsofbitches." But he said it not with anger but with a sense of wonder.

"Their hanging him shows Red Wolf's got some kind of a sense of humor," Fargo pointed out. "Though grim. Do you know him, Hank?"

"No. Looks to be a trapper." The old man nodded toward two traps that Fargo had picked up near the body.

"Did they find the dead Indian maybe?" Sally asked, "And is this their vengeance?"

"Couldn't have got here that quick anyway," Fargo told her. "No. It's a warning. Keep out of our land." He looked squarely at the two women. "And that's how we'll take it—as a warning. Just don't forget what you've seen."

They pursued the trail now, Fargo leading. As he topped a slight rise, the trail narrowed to little more than a ridge, with barely room enough for his horse. On one side was the sheer rise of the mountain piling up above them, and on the other a steep drop of a couple hundred feet to the ravine below.

Turning in his saddle to Sally, who was just behind him, he saw her chalk-white face as her horse moved forward. The buckskin was looking down at his feet, his head bent to the trail, snorting, his lion-colored ears straight out sideways, wondering whether the footing was safe.

"Don't look down," Fargo said to the girl. "Let your pony handle it. Don't do anything, and stop holding your breath."

Frightened as she was, she still flushed angrily as she saw his eyes studying her bosom.

"I'm looking at your breathing, goddammit, not your tits! Stop flattering yourself!"

It was what she needed. Her anger swept courage back into her as she glared at him.

The others were following directly behind, Hank bringing up the rear. The trail curved slightly around the side of the high rock formation. And now they discovered that ahead of them lay even narrower footing—and now without the mountain on one side. On both sides of them was a sheer drop into the ravine. The ridge was about fifty yards long, disappearing in a grove of trees on the other side.

"We're not going to cross that damn thing!" Frannie's words were the first that had been spoken in several minutes.

"Unless you want to do it at night," Fargo said grimly. "Come on. We'll do it the same as the other. Just follow me."

Fargo rode loose in the saddle yet with his attention straight as a string, his body attuned to every movement of the Ovaro, who was as surefooted as a bighorn sheep on the razorback trail. They were not a horse and a rider; they were one.

He dismounted on the other side, and when Sally reached him he saw the tension in her neck and arms. As she drew rein he reached up to help her out of the saddle. For a moment she was against him as he held her, feeling her shaking.

"Let it out," he said gently. "Let it all out."

All at once she realized where she was and pushed away from him. "I don't need that."

"I think you do," he answered simply. But he left her and turned to Frannie, who made the crossing without trouble. Finally, Hank rode the sorrel mare across without a tremor, at one point even cockily letting fly a big gob of spit into the ravine.

They rested now in the grove of ash and spruce, the ordeal over. Fargo watched Frannie's shoulders trembling.

"You hold tight like that, it's bound to make you shake," he told her.

"My God," muttered Frannie. "I don't ever— *ever*—want to do that again!"

A wheeze and croak suddenly erupted from Hank, and a rumbling sound began to gargle in his throat. Fargo realized the old man was chuckling. "Told you it was a tough trail."

And Fargo watched the grin spreading into the old hostler's eyes. "I took you at your word, Hank, that this is the only way in."

"That is correct, Trailsman, that is what I told you." He paused, rattling and whistling. "And it is the only way out."

6

They rode slowly through blasted trees, black-ened rocks and rotted logs. Evidently a fire had swept the whole side of the mountain, and not very long before. Stumps and dead trees, charred logs and black roots thrusting up through the singed earth created the blasted vista around them.

Now and again the smell of ash tinted the air. The horses didn't like it. They moved warily through the burnt land, their feet hesitant, eyes stiff with caution, their long ears spread straight out to the sides, nostrils dilating as they snorted, feeling their way under the prodding of their riders.

Finally they came to the limit of the burned-out area and entered a dense stand of hemlock, fir and spruce. Fargo led them up the steep trail that wound along the side of the mountain, while above them, getting closer, they could all see the giant rimrocks standing in the great blue sky.

"Franc's Peak," Hank said after a while,

pulling alongside Fargo, who was squinting upward.

"It's under there, is it?"

"Most couldn't find it if they spent a year looking; it's that well hid."

They rode more slowly now, at certain points getting down from their horses to lead them. Now they were out in the open again, following no trail at all but moving through thick sagebrush, the odor sharp and tangy in the hot afternoon.

Shortly after, they entered the trees again, and the horses picked their way carefully along the overgrown trail. Then, breaking into a clearing, they quickened their pace.

"They smell water," Fargo said to Sally, who had ridden up just behind him.

"I'll be glad for that," she admitted, just as they turned down a short incline and saw a spring rising out of a cutbank.

Someone had built a wooden box to catch the water. It was full and the water overflowed down the trail. They dismounted, and using their hat brims as dippers, all drank deeply.

"I've certainly never tasted water like that," Frannie said. Like all of them, she was perspiring, and Fargo noted her shirt was almost glued to her, outlining her springy bust, the nipples sticking out like little fingertips. Her eyes danced as she caught him looking.

"Best drink there is," Fargo said agreeably,

and he turned his attention to the horses, who had their noses buried in the water.

Presently Fargo said, "We want to get there before dark, so let's move it." He turned to Hank. "Looks to me like it's straight through there."

"That's it."

"Then we'll swing up to the top of that coulee yonder and come around from the other side."

The hostler licked his lips.

It was getting toward the late afternoon as they rode down the near side of the big draw and then started up the other, higher side, the trees giving way suddenly where they had been cut down.

"I can see Burl Boden didn't encourage visitors," Fargo said. "At least ones he couldn't see."

The old man chuckled. "Burl thought of everything. He wouldn't of trusted his mother. I mind him saying, 'Don't trust nobody but yourself, then you'll know who betrayed you.' " He paused to spit, cough and sniff. " 'Course that notion didn't help him any when he was taken."

"Somebody talked on him, did they?" Fargo asked. "I don't see him as a man making a dumb mistake."

"Somebody run his loose mouth," Hank replied. "Somebody named Stacey; I would bet a good stake on it."

There was no time for further conversation, for they were getting close, and Fargo signaled for complete quiet as they moved up the long side of the coulee. He was glad the sun was at their backs and not in their eyes.

About halfway up the draw he told them to stop and dismount, while he got down from the Ovaro; taking his field glasses and the Sharps, he walked up to a big bush at the rim of the draw above them. It afforded perfect cover, and he reasoned it must have grown there since Boden's time. Lying on his belly, he looked out as the whole view broke into the endless sky. It was like being at the very top of the world. Then he looked down.

He was looking at a flat area of land hidden in tall timber, at three log cabins and half a dozen sheds, some with lean-tos. There was a round horse corral with two of the bars down, the gate open and sagging. There had been a severe runoff of water from the rocks above and a swath had cut right down through, carrying logs, rocks and rubble right up to one of the log buildings, which, he saw now, was a barn. Clearly the place was deserted and had been for some time.

Not far from the barn, on a slight rise of ground, stood an unpainted outhouse. Around it some bushes grew.

The main house, the biggest, was built of dead logs, with the ends coped—scooped out in a semicircle so that they lay snugly over each other at the corners, allowing rainwater to run off instead of entering the building. The other cabin, probably a bunkhouse, and the barn were built of unpeeled logs with the ends of each log notched so that they fit one another in a right angle at the corners. The main cabin and bunkhouse had wood chinking between the logs, but the chinking on the barn was manure. All three cabins had sod roofs. The sheds and lean-tos were ramshackle and some were barely standing.

Fargo heard a jay call and saw an eagle soaring down through the great valley below, following the line of the coursing river into the south country.

Was Boden there? If he had come back, then wouldn't that verify the existence of a cache of money? Hidden where? Presumably only Boden knew, while the others—Stacey and the boys and Greenough and Kite—were waiting to follow him to it. But maybe there wasn't a cache? Maybe Boden would never show up at all or had even been here and gone. That would make the trail to John Logan stone cold. For who else would know anything, if not Burl Boden. Surely, Fargo reasoned, surely Boden would have had time to get to Hangtown from Laramie, judging by the date of the newspaper clipping. It occurred to him suddenly that maybe the Shoshone had got him, just as they had the old trapper they'd hanged and shot full of arrows.

But Boden was clearly the only possible link so far to John Logan. While Fargo had given Hank and the others he had spoken to a full description—height, weight, age—it was unfortunately a description that most of them said could fit half the population of the West.

When he was satisfied that no life was down there in the place that had been known as Hangtown, he dropped back down the draw to where the others were waiting for him. Quickly he told them what he had seen.

"I'm going down there. In a few minutes it'll be just about dusk," he said. "If anyone's about, it'll be difficult for them to spot me then, and I'll still have a little daylight to take a look around."

Squinting at the sky, he said, "Might as well be just about now." And without waiting for any response, he mounted the Ovaro. Looking down at them from the saddle, he said, "I might be there awhile, so don't look for me. Stay here." He paused, looking up toward the bullberry bush at the top of the coulee. "Hank, you cover me from there with the Sharps. He pulled the big gun out of its saddle scabbard and handed it to the old hostler. "You two cover our backtrail."

Sally was standing near his stirrup, looking up at him. "Was there—I don't suppose there was any sign of . . . I know there couldn't be. But I—I had to ask."

"Your father?" He shook his head. He had seen the strain in her face, which she had been bravely controlling all this time. "No, but I'll be looking." He waited, looking down at the top of her head, until she looked up again and he smiled gently at her. Turning the Ovaro, he started up the long incline at an angle, switching back just below the top so that he came out about a hundred yards from the bullberry bush.

Riding loose, but with every nerve and muscle keened to the action, with his eyes never leaving the scene below or the surrounding tree line, the Trailsman quartered down the long slope to Hangtown.

Dusk moved in quickly, washing over the buildings without a sound, smoothing out the day for the dark to come in and lie down.

Fargo rode into the round horse corral, dismounted and wrapped the reins loosely around a corral pole. Then he walked into the barn.

The ceiling was low, and the rubble from the washout had partially filled the doorway, so that when he stepped through, his head almost touched the roof. It wasn't a big barn. There would have been room for four horses. It was almost totally dark and he struck a wooden match and lighted his candle stub to take a look. The manger was hanging away from the log wall. It had been chewed a good bit by horses wanting salt. But long ago. Suddenly he heard a pack rat scurrying somewhere under the bottom logs; these were slightly raised from the ground, lying on stone corners.

Next he entered a tack room at one end of the barn. It smelled of old leather, oil and dirt. Old harnesses and saddle rigging, an aged saddle mildewed and chewed by pack rats, were scattered about. Some saddle blankets that were almost totally destroyed lay on a wooden rack. A can of tobacco stood on a bench. And there were rusted horseshoes, nails, a double-bitted ax with several nicks, a two-handed saw, a rotted lariat rope. Dust, dirt was on everything. As he turned, his big hat was enveloped by a cobweb.

Out in the corral he simply stood stock still for several moments listening to the land, to the rhythm of the nightfall, trying to catch any change in tempo that might signal someone's presence. There was nothing. He looked up at the bison head on top of the corral gate, backgrounded by the velvet evening sky. Then he checked the sheds, finding nothing save some shell casings. He looked into the bunkhouse, the door of which had fallen in. Nothing. The outhouse was a two-seater, and save for a disintegrated newspaper, there was nothing there. Then he walked to the main cabin.

It was long, low. It was dark inside when he pushed in the door and entered. He stood still for a moment before he lit the candle, listening, taking in the life of the deserted cabin. There was the distinct smell of unused years, animal droppings, coal oil, dried wood and sawdust and salt. There was a lamp, but he used his candle, not wanting to allow the smell of coal oil to change the atmosphere.

The cabin consisted of three rooms in a single line—kitchen, main room, bedroom. In the kitchen a range filled one of the short walls. There was firewood, some pots and pans, the usual kitchen things. A table, chairs. In the middle room some broken furniture, a potbellied jumbo stove—cold, with dead ashes inside. He sifted through, finding nothing. In the bedroom an old, broken bed, a chair. And as in the other rooms, dust everywhere. He stood wondering, filled with a strange sense of something unreal. It wasn't his danger sense, but a feeling he had on occasion when he felt he was missing something. And so he waited, standing in the center of the bedroom, the candlelight flickering on the chair and the bed, throwing dancing shadows on the log walls, which were covered with blaze marks in the dead wood. The light also worked a mysterious pattern on the dirt floor and on the sawed, upended logs that supported the bed, which was without legs, and on the dirty tarpaulin beneath it.

But Fargo was wise enough not to force the strange feeling. He would let it work on him; he knew from experience that was the best way.

When he went outside, the sky was filled with stars. He had taken the precaution of keeping his burnt match in his pocket, and so there wasn't a trace of his having entered the cabin.

He stood looking up at the sky, then started to walk around the cabin. The back of the log house was close to a high cutbank, the usual way to build in that part of the country to afford as much protection from the weather as possible. And another reason was right in front of him now; the door of a root cellar cut right into the bank of earth. He tried the door, but it wouldn't budge. Evidently some of the earth had caved in on the other side, blocking it from opening. He waited again, listening to the silence. Then he mounted the Ovaro.

Fifteen minutes later he had rejoined Hank and the two women.

In the early dawn, with the sun not yet above the far peaks, Fargo awakened gently and quickly, as had become his habit over the years. Like an animal, like an Indian or mountain man, a man living close to himself and nature who simply with the lift of an eyelid was at once totally awake in every part of the body.

He felt his hand on the burly handle of the Navy Colt, felt the air and rising light touching his face. He rose, stretched and felt the life coursing through his strong, eager body as he looked out over the long valley.

He was right up beneath the rimrocks, high above the still not visible little meadow Hank the hostler had told him about, where the Boden gang had grazed their horses "in the old days."

The previous night, after investigating the cabins at Hangtown, he had returned to the camp where Hank and the women were still awake. They'd listened in silence to his account of how he had found nothing that would indicate the presence of Boden. While he was describing the cabins and barn, he had felt Sally's eyes on him, but he only looked directly at her when he'd finished. She was staring at him with round eyes, her brow tight with anticipation as she hung on his words, examining them, it seemed, for the slightest news of her father.

"Can we go down and take a look in the morning?" she'd asked eagerly. "There could be something of his I might recognize—if he was here, I'd know it more easily than you would."

Before answering, he glanced over at Frannie. She was watching him seriously but evidently had nothing to say. Then he turned back to Sally.

"I want you to stay here. It looks to me like we'll be getting visitors down there. It'd be best for us to see them and not let them see us."

"But why!" she burst out. "We could go down and see much better in full daylight what's there. Six eyes are better than two."

"Not if they only look and don't see," he threw back at her. "I need you here. I'm not going to be around today."

She sat glowering at him, her lips clamped together, her whole body tight as a whip.

"I'll be back maybe by late forenoon," he went on. "But if it's later, you wait." He looked at each of the women in turn, letting the words sink in. "You've got weapons, ammo, grub. And you've got your horses. I'm not fooling. All right, we're looking for Boden so we can talk to him, maybe get a line on your father; but there are others who are after that cache of money, and some will kill for it."

He saw how disappointed Sally was and wasn't surprised when she asked in a demanding tone of voice, "Where are you going?"

"I have something I want to check out."

"Down there? At those cabins?"

He didn't answer but stood up to show that he was finished talking and strode out to where he had left his bedroll, signaling Hank to follow him.

"You keep close to them," he said when they were out of earshot.

Then he'd told the old hostler again to keep the horses ready. "Don't strip them. You might want to leave in a hurry; I'll be able to track you if you have to take off."

Something like a grin had come into Hank's face. "Didn't realize how much I'd been missing the action, Trailsman. I do appreciate it."

Now, up near the rimrocks, as he checked his weapons and the Ovaro's rigging, he recalled how the hostler had still maintained that there was only the one way in and one way out of Hangtown. And he had added that maybe somebody afoot could make it over the rimrocks, but never with a horse, and never without being seen.

But Fargo could simply not believe that a man of the caliber of Burl Boden would lock himself into a hideout with only one escape route. It just didn't make any sense at all. At the same time, he could see why the outlaw would let everyone think that was the only way.

In the sparkling light he rode the Ovaro along a deer trail just below the rimrocks, easing down through the timber. It was slow going, the trail hard as iron, with now and again slippery footing.

The big horse picked his way slowly, always careful of his feet. Now and then, Fargo dismounted and led him.

The trees were thick overhead, yet every so often he stopped and looked up to see the blue sky through the high, arching branches, the whispering leaves. As he came lower he heard the cries of a bluebird, a meadowlark. He saw mountain lilies and asked himself what it was that had bothered him in the log cabin.

It was very hot. He was glad when he heard the water, watched the Ovaro prick up his ears and felt the freshness in his eager gait.

Entering the little clearing, he saw a meadowlark rising from an aspen thicket, while off to his right his eye caught the rear end of a mule deer bounding away into the trees.

But the clearing was not yet the meadow; and he didn't cross it. He kneed the Ovaro and they rode around the edge close to the trees until they reached the little creek on the far end. He paused again to listen, and only when he was sure there was no one, he dismounted.

When the horse had finished drinking, Fargo let him crop the dry, crisp grass, while he studied the banks of the creek. There were a lot of stones along the banks, making it difficult to pick up signs. But he kept at it. Only when he had covered a good bit of ground did he finally spot the hoof print.

It was clearly the print he had seen near the body of the dead Shoshone. He continued, searching the ground, the bushes, the trees. And at last he was rewarded as his eye found the small piece of cloth caught in a chokecherry bush. There was no question that the red stain on it was blood.

It was shortly before noon when, following the tracks of the wounded rider and horse, Fargo and the Ovaro suddenly and with total unexpectedness—as Hank had predicted—came to the little meadow. The expanse of lush green grass lay like a jewel within the circle of hemlock and spruce, pine and fir. Fargo drew rein, and the big horse was immediately eager to drop his head to the sweet grass, but his rider held the reins; he wanted him on the alert. And so they both waited motionless and silent just inside the trees at the edge of the sunlit meadow.

It was clear to the Trailsman now that there was another trail into Hangtown, for the rider he was tracking had come from a quite different direction than he and the two women and Hank had. He had been tempted to backtrail the rider, to see just where he had crossed the ravine, but had decided it was more important to follow right on, since clearly the wounded man was heading toward Hangtown. And moreover, it was not at all unlikely that it could be Burl Boden. Who else would know the other trail?

Now, taking his position from Franc's Peak, he realized that he was almost at Hangtown, on the other side from where he had entered when he'd checked out the cabins.

And suddenly, over there, cropping the soft green grass, stomping at flies, his tail and mane swishing, was a chunky, blaze-faced dun horse with two white-stockinged legs. He was still saddled and bridled, the bit jangling as he cropped grass or raised his head to shake away flies. He was hobbled, feeding along the side of the meadow, almost into the trees where it was not easy to spot him. There was a Winchester in the saddle boot.

Fargo, wary of a trap, rode the Ovaro around through the trees until he was close to the dun horse. It was easy to catch him. With the rawhide hobbles he couldn't run away. Holding him by his cheek strap, gentling him and talking, Fargo slowly slipped his hand onto the dun's rump and down his left rear leg. When he lifted the leg he found the loose shoe he was looking for.

And where was the rider? If Hank the hostler hadn't known of this other trail, then the chances were it was a secret known only to Boden. But that was slippery, he knew. Whoever it was it looked as though he was the one who had shot the Shoshone; the dun's hoof print was clear on that. Then he had ridden to the meadow, knowing how to come in toward Hangtown from an unknown direction. So he would be there—at Hangtown, or nearby. He could, Fargo realized, be very near by.

He began working at the edge of the meadow

123

near the dun horse, but at first found nothing, for the dun had of course moved around, though it couldn't go far because of the hobbles. But shortly he was rewarded by finding the grass bent, as though someone had dragged something—or himself?—through it. And then he saw the man. He was lying down, partially supported by a fallen tree. Fargo squatted, peered into the cold face. It was the man who had spoken to him across the street from the Buffalo Horn Hotel on the afternoon of the women's auction. It was the man named Tyson Titchener. He was dead.

Careful to leave no sign of his own presence, Fargo studied him. He had been shot in the back and chest, and not too long ago. Yes, Titchener; and Fargo saw he was still carrying the hideout gun he'd spotted in Washing Springs. But at his right hip he wore an empty holster. From his papers Fargo learned that he was a bounty hunter. He supposed that was why Titchener had wanted to speak to him the other day. Next Fargo untied the war bag from the saddle skirt on the dun. In it were cards, a half-empty bottle of whiskey, some Indian jewelry and moccasins. Not much to have won in a game costing a man's life. But Titchener could have been drinking.

There were two bullets fired from the hideout and Fargo reasoned that the Shoshone had shot Titchener with the Colt he'd won gambling after Titchener had fired the hideout, which had not killed the Indian instantly. Evidently Titchener's second shot had done the trick, while the Colt had been lost along the way.

Evidently looking for Boden and Hangtown, Titchener had made it this far. Maybe he had stumbled on the trail coming up to the meadow; maybe someone had told him. At any rate, he had been getting weaker and weaker from loss of blood, and staggered and crawled into the trees and died.

It was late afternoon when Fargo rode the Ovaro out of the meadow. He was leading the dun horse with the dead man strapped across the saddle.

Yet he was still puzzling over the question of John Logan as he rode back to the campsite where he had left the two girls and old Hank. Logan had as good as disappeared. Had he gotten himself into the pen? Was he even alive? And had he been working with Burl Boden? Surely he wouldn't have mentioned Hangtown in a letter to his wife if he'd not been there. Hangtown wasn't the kind of place you mentioned casually, as sort of visiting or passing through. And yet, if he'd been a member of the gang, he would never have mentioned the place.

He might have quite casually gotten involved in the robberies, though perhaps not at the time he wrote his wife. Could it have been something like that? Maybe later, after the letter, he had gotten involved; or he might even have left that part of the country, only been around Hangtown a very short time.

The three were eating cold venison that Fargo had shot back along the trail when he rode in with the dead man tied across the dun horse.

They stopped their conversation the moment he appeared and now crowded around him as he got down from the pinto. He noticed Sally in particular as she stared at the body, her face white, her hands tense as she brought them to her face.

He knew she was wondering if it might be her father and so he said right away, "It's a man named Titchener. I found him back in the meadow you told me about, Hank."

"Who is he?" the old man croaked.

"Bounty hunter, I believe. He was after Boden, I guess, but he looks like the one shot the Shoshone."

Fargo was untying the lariat rope and now he nodded to Hank to give him a hand lowering the body to the ground.

"Who shot him?" The old man was wheezing from the exertion of handling the dead weight.

"Looks like the Shoshone. But . . ." Fargo let it hang, for he was suddenly struck again by the sense of something not quite seen, something he might have been missing. It was the same feeling he'd had when he was standing in the bedroom of the cabin down in Hangtown. And yet all the pieces seemed to fit. Then what was it that kept him going over it again?

The exertion of carrying the dead man and laying him on a blanket a good distance from their campsite was hard on the old hostler, who fell into a coughing attack, which caused him to bend almost double as he struggled for air. Finally he straightened up and stood there, weaving a little on his feet, looking down at the dead eyes of Tyson Titchener.

Fargo picked up an end of the blanket and rolled the body in it. "In the morning we'll pack him down to one of the cabins and hope the rats don't get him. Then when we get back to town, we'll tell the law."

"Greenough."

"That's the size of it."

Fargo felt the girl standing behind him, and he turned to face her. "I don't guess all this is the way you expected."

"I don't know, Fargo. I don't understand why no one seems to have heard of my father. John Burleigh Logan, it's a very simple name. It's not complicated, hard to pronounce. I don't know. I really just don't know. . . ." And she stood there shaking her head in despair. "I'm beginning to ask myself what I'm doing out here. Why did I come?"

"Why did you?"

"Well, I said it was to find my father. But it's almost as though something, some kind of fate or something, just doesn't want me to find him."

"I suggested to you once that maybe he doesn't want to be found. Maybe he's happy in a whole new life."

"But he wrote Mother telling her he missed all of us and loved us . . . and all that. . . ."

"Man can change his mind."

He watched her taking that in, and then after a short silence she said, "So can a woman change her mind." She was looking at him calmly. And then she said, "Forgive me. I'm a bit unstrung. When I saw that body, I had the terrible thought that it was him, my—my dad." She started to turn away, but then as something struck her she almost spun back to face him. "I want to go down and look through those buildings myself in the morning."

"Look, we're going to have to get out of here early. We're overdue for a visit from Greenough and Johnson, or Stacey and his boys, or both. There's no point in hanging around for that."

"But we came out to see this man Boden or anyone else who might be living out here."

"Well, you met the man hanging from the cottonwood and you've met this man here, and I'd say that's about the size of the population around here. Now all those others are coming out to see if they can find Boden's cache, and they are not going to want anyone else in the way. Kite Johnson is also coming out to get even with you. You want to hang around for that? I don't." And he added, "And not to forget the Shoshones. They'll have for sure found that body by now."

He saw the anger whip into her face and he thought she was even going to hit him. "We'll start before it's light," he told her. "So you be ready. Tell Frannie."

* * *

He was sitting on his bedroll, ready to turn in, but had taken a moment to look to the west, toward the great shadows of the farther mountains in the velvet sky. Hearing something, he turned his head. The quarter moon offered enough light to see her approaching.

"Do you feel like company?"

"I do indeed."

"I missed you, Fargo."

"Well, I'm here now," he said, slipping his arm around her.

What he liked about Frannie was that she didn't waste time with formalities. And she certainly didn't now as she dropped her clothes and swung her leg around him, pushing him down on his back. Expertly she undressed him, yanking his shorts away from his giant erection and then, still on top of him, straddling it, rubbing her bush up and down its full length while he guided it just inside the pink wet lips, refusing to go deeper as they tantalized each other.

"Give it to me from behind, Fargo. . . ." she gasped as she swung off him and crouched on hands and knees. He mounted her from the rear.

"Fargo . . . dear God . . . oh my God . . . ah, aieeee!"

Reaching under her now, he took each big mound in his hands, squeezing, tickling the hard, erect nipples, still rubbing his organ against her bush while she cried out in ecstasy. "Give it to me now, come with me now . . .

Fargo! I, I have to have it. Fargo, dear God, please, please, Fargo, fuck me. . .!"

And Fargo drove into her as she cried out, her buttocks thrashing as she started walking on hands and knees over his bedroll; he pumped his charging maleness up into the center of her body until finally she could bear no more and pulled away, turning onto her back. He thrust into her, spearing her with his enormous joy stick, stroking faster and faster and tighter as she gasped and bucked and thrashed out her passion as he joined her in the ultimate instant of sweetness.

When she had gone he lay on his back. Though he felt relaxed, sleep would not come. There was still that nagging at the edges of his mind. Boden. Stacey and the boys. Kite. Clyde Greenough. They'd all be converging on Hangtown any time now. And the master of Hangtown? Where was he? Maybe there was no cache and he'd taken off for California. Of course, it also depended on whether they could all get through the Shoshones. There was no doubt in his mind that the best thing for himself and his three companions would be to cut out fast.

He still couldn't sleep, and he reasoned it was just as well. He needed to be alert. The thought made him feel better, helped to ease the dissatisfaction that gripped him.

He heard steps coming through the underbrush. Not Hank. Frannie returning for more?

The moon was fading when Sally came into his line of vision.

"What can I do for you, honey? You lonely?" He was lying on his back, naked but for his shorts. Now he rose up on his elbows and looked at her, fully aware of how she resolutely avoided looking at his bare body.

He felt rather than saw her taking a grip on herself. "I wanted to talk to you about my father."

"What about him?"

"Fargo, I—I've got to keep looking. Will you help me? You say there's nothing in those buildings, that they've been deserted for years." She paused, and he watched her forehead tighten. "I'd thought . . . I'd hoped we'd find somebody out here to talk to. Some sort of clue. Can't we go down before we leave here? Maybe—just maybe—there's something in one of the cabins. Something of my dad's. I mean—maybe he was a member of Boden's gang. An—an outlaw."

There was something in her appeal that was new. A fresh tone. Somehow she had lost some of her arrogance; somehow she seemed to have grown in a certain way.

"Fargo, I really must see those buildings. I just feel if my dad lived here, worked here with Boden and those people, there'd have to be some trace."

"It's all dust," he said. "Dust and cobwebs." And then as he heard the words he had just spoken he knew his instinct had been right. It had been right in front of him the whole time. He turned to the girl. "We'll go down when it's light," he said. "Now go get some sleep."

But she didn't move. She stood there looking down at him.

"Thank you," she said simply. "And Fargo—I—I want to say I'm sorry about how I've been sometimes. I guess I just was pretty nervous about this whole thing. It—it got to be a little too much. I've even begun to wonder whether I've been doing the right thing."

She was standing with her thumb knuckle at her mouth, like a child, he thought. In one flowing movement he was on his feet, aware of his erection almost bursting his shorts as he put his arms around her. She suddenly let her head lie against his naked chest, and he felt tears.

"Come lie down," he said. "You'll feel better."

"No, Fargo. I'm not ready. Not yet." And she pushed away, and turning, ran down the path to where she had her bed.

After she'd gone he lay on the bed trying to let his passion subside. Presently, he remembered the moment when he had stood in the barn with the cobwebs all over his big black Stetson hat.

7

They were lying on the bank, protected by the juniper bush, looking down at the two approaching horsemen.

"Who do you reckon?" Hank asked, his wheezing breath like a file in the thin air.

Fargo grunted, his hand loose on the Sharps. "Greenough and Kite. Maybe Stacey. Hard to say, but we'll know directly."

"So long as it ain't them Shoshone devils. You think Boden will come?"

"He's already here," Fargo said.

Hank's breath whistled abruptly past his dry lips as he turned to stare at Fargo. "How'n hell you figger that, Trailsman?"

"It was looking me right in the face the whole time, only I didn't see it right away." But he didn't explain it. There was no time. "Right now I want you to cut back to the meadow. Take the horses. Leave the dun, but keep him out of sight."

"Where you want me to take the animals?"

"I was scouting out there this morning early. I

put a marker for you. You go out past the buildings and follow the trail right to the edge of the meadow. Doesn't take but a few minutes, because you'll be moving fast. When you get to the meadow, go to your left along the edge, inside the trees, so anybody coming in can't see the animals. There's a dead log lying against a stump."

The old man was nodding his whole body as he followed the instructions. Fargo continued, "About the distance from here to the barn after you get to the meadow."

"Got'cha."

"Tie them in the trees, well out of sight. Then get back here."

"Where will you be?"

"Probably in the house, but don't come in unless I call you. And look out for our visitors when you come back."

He had started toward the cabins, which were a couple of hundred yards from where he and Hank had been watching the two riders. Hank was some yards ahead of him, limping, dragging his game leg, but moving fast even so, when Fargo called to him, "Where are the women?"

"I just seen 'em go into the cabin," the hostler called back.

Cursing under his breath, Fargo started toward the cabin. He had told Sally definitely not to go inside without him. He was there in another moment and without hesitating opened the door, and froze on the threshold.

The shotgun with the twin barrels cut down was pointed right at him, while the two girls were standing, staring at the man who was seated in one of the deer-covered chairs. He was medium-sized, about sixty, with dark hair, a lined, trail-weathered face but with a suspicious pallor that Fargo recognized. His sparkling gray eyes seemed almost to be laughing at the shock he was causing the two women. He held the scattergun firmly in his left hand with his forefinger on the trigger. His right arm and hand were wrapped in a shirt which was evidently serving as a bandage.

"I'm afraid I frightened the young ladies, sir. But won't you all sit down. There are chairs. And—uh . . ." The smile touched the corners of his mouth as the gray eyes lighted up even more. "I see we can expect some more guests shortly."

Fargo had dropped his right hand to his side. "Sorry I wasn't here to greet you myself, Mr. Boden," he said, with a glance toward the bedroom.

"Ah—so you figured it out." The smile filled his face, but Fargo noted that not for an instant did the old outlaw cease his strict vigilance. "How?" he asked.

"No cobwebs." And as the girls turned to him in surprise, he said, "There are cobwebs everywhere. Except there weren't in the bedroom."

The man in the chair shifted as the women seated themselves, while Fargo remained standing. "A bit difficult getting up through the passage with this." And he bent his gray head

135

slightly toward his bandaged arm. "I was pleased to find the old tunnel was still holding up after all these years. I had it built by good men."

"And the root cellar?" Fargo asked.

"A little cramped, but good enough for a hideout; especially for my present purposes."

He was looking at Sally and Frannie. "I'm only sorry that the young ladies have to be here when our visitors arrive."

Sally had not taken her eyes off the man in the chair. Suddenly she spoke, "Are you . . . uh . . ."

"Burl Boden, miss, at your service."

"Can you tell me, do you know a man named John Logan?" She was almost stammering. "I'm his daughter, Sally Logan."

Fargo was watching Boden's face carefully and was certain he saw something move behind it. Only for a split second, and then the hard, cynical look was back, along with the slightly baiting tone of voice. Yet there had been that instant of—something else.

"You look like Johnnie Logan," he said.

"You knew my father?" And her face shone.

"We did some business together some years ago. I liked him. I even—uh—asked him to join my line of work. But he wouldn't. He was a good man. An honest man."

"And now—now? I've come all the way from Missouri to try to find him. Can you tell me—anything? Where he is?"

"I don't have a notion where John Logan is. I

haven't seen him in years." He paused, looking at her carefully. "I'm real sorry, miss."

"Thank you," she murmured, and dropped her eyes to her lap, her mouth working in disappointment; her hopes had lifted only to be cruelly dashed.

Boden turned to the Trailsman. "You're not the law. I don't see any tin star. You a bounty hunter?" The words were as hard as the barrels of the shotgun whose twin holes were still pointing at Fargo.

"The name is Fargo. Skye Fargo. I'm just helping the young lady to locate her father."

"That right?" He pointed his chin at Sally.

"Yes—it's the truth." Fargo caught the fear in her voice, and he appreciated old Hank's description of Burl Boden.

"And you?" Boden looked at Frannie.

"I'm a friend of Sally's. We came out here together from Missouri." She managed a smile. "You really scared us when you just walked in from the bedroom like that."

"Those riders will be here any minute," Boden said, lowering the shotgun. "I got no argument with you, Fargo. You want to stay inside or out? I'm keeping the ladies, just for my own welfare. You understand. If those visitors are who I think they are, then there's liable to be lead flying. You girls get down on the floor."

"It's Greenough and Kite Johnson." Fargo was watching at the window as the two horsemen rode up.

"Don't know 'em."

"They're after the girls . . . and also after you. Greenough is the law." Fargo had his back to Boden and was still looking out the window. "Who killed the Shoshone, Boden? Was that you, or was it Titchener?"

"Titchener? He that bounty feller?"

Fargo turned back to face the man in the chair. "Clever the way you rode him in on the same horse and left it like he was alone, and the one who'd shot the Shoshone."

Burl Boden grinned. "I never deny anything, Fargo. But I do admire the way you figure things out. Wish I'd had you with me in the old days."

They heard a loud whinny outside, and a voice shouted at the cabin. "Anybody in there! This is United States Deputy Marshal Clyde Greenough. Open up! This is the law!"

And then they all heard Hank the hostler, his voice croaking yet louder than they had ever heard it before. "Fargo, there is a bunch riding in fast! Let me in!"

"That's Hank used to be in your gang, Boden," Fargo said as he drew his gun and stepped quickly to the door. The man in the chair nodded. "Hank Wagner? I know him. But Fargo, I am covering that door. Anybody tries to get in except Hank will be cut right in two with this load of blue whistlers! Or if you try to get out," he added. He had the cut-down 12-gauge in his left hand and it was pointed right at Fargo. "You women lie down flat on the floor—right now! I told you already!"

As Fargo opened the door Hank charged in, followed by a round of firing that splattered into the log walls but hit nobody.

"That was a warning!" Greenough shouted. "Next time we're aiming lower! Now open up!"

"Jesus H. Christ—Burl!" The old man's face was split in a grin from ear to ear, as he almost fell, gasping and wheezing into the cabin.

"Hank, you old buzzard. Don't come close, I got to keep this man covered."

"Fargo—he's all right." The old man was shaking with excitement.

"I know. I didn't tell him to unbuckle. But those sonsofbitches will start ventilating this place directly, it sounds like."

"Burl, it's Dutch Stacey out there with a dozen men, maybe more."

"Stacey!" Boden's face was a mask. "I knew that sonofabitch would show up." He threw his eyes at Fargo, who was watching from the side of the window to see how the horsemen were deploying themselves.

"Fargo, do those girls know what all those sonsofbitches out there are after?"

"Your cache? They know."

"And you?"

Fargo shrugged. "I told you what I'm here for."

"Anybody gets that cache—I mean if there is a

cache—it'll be over somebody's dead body. And it won't be mine."

"I don't want that money, Boden. I want to get those women out of here. Hank can take them through the tunnel while we cover."

"Take 'em. Good luck to you, Fargo whoever-you-are." As he spoke a fusillade of firing drove against the log house.

"The tunnel connects through the root cellar—that right?"

"There's a barrel stuck in the wall. Pull out the lid and you crawl through. It's a good ways but you should come out clear. That's how I got in here—what the hell!"

"By God, there's rifles all over," wheezed old Hank, as another wave of bullets struck the front of the cabin, taking out two windows.

Suddenly a voice reached them. "Boden! We've got you surrounded. Come out with your hands up!"

"They want you alive, naturally," Fargo said as he snatched up the Sharps.

"I know," the outlaw snapped. He had risen from his chair, the shotgun still in his left hand. "I'll cover this side."

Fargo said, "We'll hold 'em while Hank gets the women through the tunnel."

"You can only go one at a time on account of the air," Boden warned.

"Does Stacey know about the tunnel?"

"Stacey knows shit," snapped the old outlaw. "That sonofabitch! I've got a score to settle with him! See, Fargo, they want me alive to get the cache. But they also want me dead. I mean Stacey and that Harold sonofabitch. But I came back just for that. Just to even it—which I am by God going to do. The stupid sonsofbitches fell for it. Did they think I wouldn't be expecting them, for Christ sake!"

. Fargo was standing at another window, waiting, listening as Boden talked. He knew that sooner or later something had to move outside.

And it did. And his shot was true. The man's scream of pain cut the air like a trumpet, but was instantly drowned in a crash of returning rifle fire. This was followed by a lull.

"Boden!" a voice called.

"That's Stacey!" croaked Hank as he started into the bedroom.

"The sonofabitch!"

"Boden, you come out, we'll let the others go. We don't want the women, or Fargo."

"The hell we don't!" shouted Kite Johnson's voice. "Those damn women owe me five hundred dollars, plus that bitch's husband wants her back. I want them women! You hear me in that fucking cabin?"

The women were still lying on the floor, as Boden had ordered them, Sally on her back, Frannie face down.

"They've got the root cellar covered!" Boden called from the other side of the room.

"The only thing is I am not sure if Stacey's men are down by the other end, where the tunnel comes out," Fargo said. "I saw them taking their horses in that direction, probably to picket."

"Shit!" Boden had dropped the shotgun and now fired his handgun at an attacker who had crept close during the lull. The man's cry attested to the outlaw's accuracy.

"Only one way to handle that," said Fargo.

"Blast away?"

"We've got to draw them in if they're out there. Otherwise Hank and the girls will run right into them."

And now a sudden barrage of rifle fire came from the attackers. Fargo and Boden fired back as the bullets tore into the cabin from three sides.

Suddenly a man screamed at the side of the house, and Boden roared, "Got the sonofabitch, by God! Fargo, we are evening it!"

"We're low on ammo, Boden."

"Got an idea?"

Fargo looked at Sally who was following Frannie into the bedroom. "Get that jug of coal oil over there, and take those shavings by the jumbo stove. Spread them along the sill."

"You gonna fire this place?"

"We'll make it through the tunnel while they're distracted with the fire." He turned to Sally. "Hurry it up."

In a few moments she had done as he'd ordered.

"Now you get started into the tunnel. Hurry! And remember, one at a time."

Another severe volley of rifle fire struck the sides of the cabin.

"Here they come with a big log on the door!"

Fargo was quickly reloading as he gave the warning.

The fury of the Sharps and Boden's Colt drove the men away. They dropped the log, scattering.

Fargo reasoned that the girls and Hank were by now started through the tunnel, maybe as far as the root cellar. "You go next, Boden. I'm going out the back window in the kitchen."

"I'm staying!" He looked at Fargo. His face was smeared with dirt, but Fargo saw the triumph in it. His eyes were gleaming. "Christ, Fargo, do you know what it's like to be in the pen!"

"I know what it's like to be free."

"That's what I'm talking about."

Another volley hit the cabin. And another.

Suddenly the firing stopped.

"I don't like it when they're that quiet," Boden said. "It means they're up to something."

"We're getting lower on ammo," Fargo warned. "And we can't fire the cabin till they get further through the tunnel."

In the silence Boden called out. "Stacey! Stacey! It's Boden!"

"What you want, Boden!" Stacey's voice came crackling across the open area in front of the cabin.

"I want to talk."

"Come on out then!"

143

"Can't. I'm shot up. You got all the others. There's no one left but me."

"You're lying!"

"I'll open the door. I'll trust you. I know what you're looking for. Well, I got to show you. It's in here. It's in the cabin, Stacey!"

There was a long silence and Fargo saw that Boden was about to call out again when they heard Stacey.

"If you're lying, Boden, I won't just kill you; I'll stake you out, Injun style. You sonofabitch, I promise you that!"

There was a wicked grin on Boden's face. "Get going, Fargo. What are you waiting for! Get into the tunnel."

"They've got to get through first. I'm going out the kitchen window just when they come in the front. There's a chance nobody will be looking that way."

"You're crazy."

"If they get caught in that tunnel, someone's got to be outside to help them."

But outside the cabin Stacey still wasn't convinced. "Boden, you're lying!" he shouted.

"I want you to let me go," Boden shouted back. "That's all! The others are dead. You want that cache, or don't you? I want to get out of here! You can have the cache. But I've got to show you where it is! Make it a deal, Stacey!"

"He needs a convincer," Fargo said. "Tell him you're firing the place."

He picked up the jug of coal oil and spread

more about the cabin, while Boden called out to Stacey.

A hurricane of bullets suddenly hit the cabin. Fargo was nicked across the back of his hand.

"I got it in the leg," Boden said, falling onto a chair, his face twisted in pain.

Fargo took a wooden match out of his shirt pocket.

"How did you figure it, Fargo? How did I fuck up?"

Fargo was holding the match, ready to strike it with his thumbnail, one-handed.

"A man who's dying—like Titchener was supposed to be doing—wouldn't take the trouble, or even be able to hobble his horse."

A wan grin crept into Boden's face. "One mistake."

"Two," Fargo said. "The way you looked at your daughter."

"She's a damn pretty girl, Fargo. Any man could look at her like that."

"I'll cover that," Fargo said, and he struck the match on his thumbnail and dropped it into the wet shavings.

"I'm going out the kitchen window. You coming?"

"Open the door before you go."

Swiftly Fargo unlocked the door of the cabin, leaving it ajar, and stepped into the kitchen.

"So long, Fargo."

"So long, Logan!"

The flames suddenly danced into the room as

145

Boden laughed. Through a crack in the log wall separating the kitchen from the other room, Fargo watched the flames leaping up, heard the shouts of the men outside and saw the wicked grin on Boden's face. He looked like an old wolf who has finally trapped his prey.

"That was you, wasn't it, turned me in to the law, huh, Stacey!" he said as the door of the cabin opened and Stacey, Harold and three men burst in.

"Tell me where that money is; I mean fast, Boden, you sonofabitch! Boys, tend to that fire!" Stacey's .45 was pointing right at Burl Boden's chest. The men were slapping their jackets at the fire, coughing as smoke began to fill the cabin.

"Dutch, I'm unarmed. And shot up to boot."

"Where's the money, dammit!"

"It's inside, Stacey, in the kitchen. It's heavy; you're going to need both hands to carry it."

Fargo saw the fire reflected in Burl Boden's sweating face.

"Boys, you get that fire out!" Stacey, half turning, roared out the desperate order as he wiped tears from his eyes.

It was at that precise moment that Burl Boden raised his bandaged arm and shot Stacey right in the belly. Stacey began to sink in agony and amazement to the floor, his eyes staring like doorknobs, his big mouth hanging open in total—final—disbelief. In that moment of finality, Burl Boden shot twice again through his bandaged hand and arm, accounting for Harold

146

and another man before a wave of bullets carried him to the floor.

"Stacey! The word was not weak. Dying, the old outlaw spoke his triumph. "Stacey, you stupid sonofabitch. You just never learned how not to be dumb!"

8

They rode mercilessly through the night, the great orange cloud of the burning log cabin lighting the sky behind them, urging them on. They stopped only when Fargo felt the need to breathe the horses. No one was tired. They were beyond fatigue, beyond exhaustion. The danger from pursuit was too great, the drama they had experienced too awesome.

Fargo had met them at the opening of the tunnel, near the place where Hank had tethered the horses. Luckily there were none of Stacey's men about, but they could come at any moment.

Fargo had them walk the horses until they were on the far side of the meadow, and only then did everyone mount. In the dark it was almost impossible to find the trail and Fargo had to call upon all of his skills to get them safely down to the bottom of the ravine and across. By the time they got that far, all were cut and bruised from being slashed by brambles, from bumping into branches and the trunks of trees in the dark; clothing was torn and Frannie received a severe scratch along the back of her arm.

On the other side of the ravine they rested, let the horses drink and bathed themselves a little as Fargo did his best to keep up their spirits.

"You figure they're coming after?" Hank asked.

"I can hear them now and again."

"How did they pick up our trail?" Frannie asked.

"Easy enough, the noise we've had to make."

"Are they close?"

"Close enough so we don't want to slow down," the Trailsman said laconically.

Some time later Fargo ordered a second halt at a clearing on top of a mesa. Even from this distance they could still see a hint of the fire that was destroying fabled Hangtown.

"The house that Burl Boden built," was how Hank put it; he stood ruminating beside Fargo as they both watched the color lighting the dark sky.

"He had the last word, Hank."

"Figures." The old man paused. "Only one thing I regret."

"What's that?"

"That I didn't get that sonofabitch Stacey."

"You wouldn't have wanted to take that pleasure from Boden, would you?"

The old man studied it a moment and then said, "No. No I wouldn't."

"There goes all that money," Frannie said with a sigh. "What a pity."

"I don't think there was any cache," Sally said. "Was there?" She turned to Fargo. "Do you think so?" It was the first she had spoken since she had left the cabin to go through the tunnel. He had watched her, her lips set in a straight line, her face pale, her shoulders taut against the strain she had been under. He wondered what she could be thinking. But he had left her alone.

Now he said, "I don't know. If it was in the cabin, then it's gone up in smoke. If not, where would anyone look?"

"I'll bet he just made up the story so he could get revenge on Stacey," Frannie said. "He was one smart man, that Burl Boden."

"But when we get to Washing Springs they'll still be after us; they'll catch up with us then," the old hostler said. "Greenough can whip up a posse, even if he waits a week on it. He's the law. And there's that sonofabitch Kite. I don't believe either of them took lead."

"Was Greenough in the gang, Hank?" Fargo asked.

The old man snorted, hawked and blew his nose between his thumb and forefinger, following this operation with a big gob of spittle aimed right into the center of a clump of sage. "There wasn't nobody around these parts in those days that wasn't mixed up with Burl, one way or the other. Clyde, he was sort of a assistant to Burl; I mean when Burl was being marshal. So he wasn't exactly in the gang, and he wasn't exactly not in it neither."

"Anyhow, he'll be after us. I believe Greenough and Johnson kept pretty much in the background at the cabin, and let Stacey do all the jawboning. And the fighting," Fargo added.

"That's Clyde Greenough. Let a man do all the hard work and then he'll come in for the cream," Hank said, holding his side where he'd banged into a tree.

"No wonder him and Kite paired up," Frannie said.

Two hours later, Fargo drew rein. In the east the sky was lightening, but the country where they were was still shrouded in night.

Sally rode the buckskin up to where Fargo was seated on the Ovaro, looking out over the plain that stretched below them. "I have a strange feeling that it's taking us even longer than necessary to get to Washing Springs. Is there anything wrong?" she asked.

He turned his head to look at her. She was tired, he could see, but she still had her spirit. Her hazel eyes seemed to shine, in spite of everything. "Nothing wrong," he said. "We'll only be stopping a little bit here."

"But that's the east, isn't it?"

He nodded. "Sun usually comes up from there." He said it in such a way that she gave a little laugh.

"The way we've been whirling around, I might easily have gotten it backward," she said lightly.

"You're not twisted around. And, yes, we have been going in a circle. I didn't tell you because I thought you'd—"

"Not try hard enough? I think you're right. Better to have us think we were getting well away."

"You're pretty sharp."

"I'm a school marm, remember? That's what a school marm gets paid for."

And they laughed together at that.

"Where are we going, Fargo?"

"Right now we're headed for the center of the Shoshone reservation. More or less. And then, Hangtown."

Hank kneed his sorrel mare closer, having overheard this last. "Trailsman! By God, have you gone plumb loco?"

It was too late for Fargo to have answered, even had he wanted to. His keen ear had caught the choppy bark of a coyote.

"They've already spotted us," he said, looking up at the sky, sniffing. It had begun to lighten more and they could distinguish shapes around them. "We're taking that trail down—yonder." He pointed. "Single file. We'll still be fairly covered because it's darker down there than up here."

Nobody questioned it and immediately he started the Ovaro down the hard trail, while the two women and Hank followed, the old man bringing up the rear. Their horses made no sound on the trail, for which Fargo was grateful, nor did they leave tracks.

In a short while they had reached the plain below and he led them into a stand of cottonwood trees.

"We've got our ass in it now, by God, Fargo," croaked old Hank as he drew alongside the Trailsman. "Mind my askin' why the hell we're heading back to Hangtown? We got the Injuns on our front and Stacey's bunch on our ass. It don't appear to me like we can go anywheres exceptin' six deep down!"

"I want you and the women to stay here in the trees. I'm going to to scout around."

And he had slipped away, making no sound as he melted into the trees.

He had heard the coyote bark again and was sure it was not four-legged. More than likely a Shoshone. The question was whether or not he was with a small party or something larger. In any event, the Indian would give the signal that there were visitors on reservation land.

Fargo fell easily into his long loping stride as he slipped through the trees until he found himself close to the area where he knew the coyote bark had come from. He stopped, listened, heard it again.

Silent as shadow now, he followed an old buffalo path for about two hundred yards, finally stopping a short distance from where he suddenly spotted three Shoshones sitting around a dying fire. They were talking and evidently listening to the scout who was signaling with the sound of the coyote.

Now he heard the bark again, off to his right, and one of the men at the fire answered.

It crossed Fargo's mind then that their signaling did not necessarily concern him and his three companions. Was it perhaps the Stacey bunch? He knew they were close; perhaps the Shoshone did too.

He waited, letting his breath out, staying low in his body, relaxing, while at the same time staying alert as he planned his next move.

Just in time he heard movement behind him, spinning and ducking as the tomahawk swished past his head. He set himself, drove a smashing blow up into his attacker's groin and followed with a kick in the stomach. As the Indian doubled over Fargo chopped his big fist under his chin. As the Shoshone hit the ground Fargo brought his heel down hard on his ear, killing him instantly.

The three at the fire were now racing toward him. Fargo had the Arkansas throwing knife out and slashed into the abdomen of the first Shoshone, who sank to his knees, vainly trying to hold his belly together.

The remaining two were on him, bringing him to the ground, one of them straddling him with a blade in his raised fist ready to strike. Fargo twisted to the left, then right, then feinted to the left and twisted right and threw off the man with the knife, kicking out at the second Indian at the same time. His heavy boot scored, knocking out

154

the Shoshone's front teeth. And then Fargo delivered a wicked chop with the side of his hand to the warrior who was still trying to stick him with his knife, hitting him just below the Adam's apple. The Indian fell on his back, grunting out his life. The final Shoshone, whose teeth had been smashed, was on his feet, running, and Fargo let him go. So far, his plan was working. The Shoshone would reach camp with the news and in a short time Red Wolf's warriors would hit the path—to confront the remains of the Stacey gang.

Quickly Fargo returned to the girls and Hank, and without a pause mounted the Ovaro. "We're heading for Hangtown." And he drew his Colt and fired a shot in the air.

"You want them to come after!" cried Hank, gargling with astonishment.

"I want to make damn sure both parties come after," he said. "After each other." He kneed the big horse, saying, "We'll meet on the other side of that big butte. Wait there for me."

He worked fast, covering their tracks; then made sure there were plenty of signs for the remains of the Stacey gang to follow to where he knew the Shoshone would be coming.

When he was satisfied with his work he cut over to the butte where Hank and the women were waiting.

They could smell the smoldering fire when they were still some distance from the cabin.

"Lucky it didn't catch in the timber," old Hank croaked.

Fargo nodded, his eyes watching the trail, making sure no one might have stayed behind. When they reached the meadow he called a halt. "Hank and I will ride in," he said to the women. "It won't be pretty to look at."

"Fargo, what are we doing here?" Sally wanted to know. "Is it just to get away from that gang and the Indians? I don't understand."

"Me and Hank," he said, cutting his eye to the old man. "We've got something to do." He looked at her. "I thought we'd bury Mr. Boden. You didn't meet up with your father exactly, but you met someone who'd known him."

"I see." Her hazel eyes were big and round as she stared at him, taking it in. Then her face cleared. "I'd like to take part in that."

"He had to be in the fire," he warned. "And there are others." He looked at the lush grass where it ran toward the creek. "Maybe here? We can bring him here."

The girl turned toward Frannie. "Could we?"

Frannie, a thoughtful look on her face, nodded.

"Wait here then," Fargo told them.

He was glad the girls weren't with them when he and Hank viewed the holocaust. The cabin was still burning, but the fire was almost out, and there was little left except charred logs. Bodies were strewn about, but to the surprise of both, Boden's body was not where Fargo had seen him

156

shot down. They were able to see where Stacey and his men had died in the cabin, though the bodies were burned beyond recognition. The odor of death and burned flesh enclosed the atmosphere, holding it like a huge mitten. Fargo felt his stomach turn, but he controlled it. Hank vomited violently. But where was Burl Boden's body?

"Jesus, Fargo, don't tell me that old outlaw pulled another trick and got away?"

Fargo didn't answer. He was looking at the root cellar. "Give me a hand, Hank."

The door was burned, too hot to touch, but they got a shovel and a pitchfork from the barn and forced it open. Burl Boden lay on his back on the dirt floor of the root cellar.

"Crawled through the tunnel before he cashed in!" Hank's unnecessary words fell nowhere as he and Fargo carried the body outside.

But old Hank couldn't handle it without speaking. "Crawled in here somehow, still trying to get out. He's hardly burned at all, by God—sure not like Stacey and them!"

"He was a tough old boy." Fargo was squatting by the body of Burl Boden, looking down at the strangely peaceful face, the hand clenched across his chest. Then, leaning forward, he began to pry open the dead man's fist.

"He's got something there," Hank croaked, his breath whistling with excitement.

It took all Fargo's strength to force open the fist and remove the slip of yellow paper. Then they wrapped the body in a horse blanket and carried it to the meadow.

With the shovel they had taken from the barn, the two of them took turns digging the grave while the women waited.

When it was all over and Burl Boden had been buried in the little meadow, Fargo said, "We'll camp on the other side of the creek. In the morning we'll head into Washing Springs."

Later, when he was currying the Ovaro, he felt Sally approaching.

"I don't know why we—you—did that, Fargo," she said simply. "But thank you." It was the first any of them had spoken since they had buried Burl Boden.

Fargo nodded, and dropping the curry comb onto the grass, he took the yellow slip of paper out of his shirt pocket and handed it to her.

"What is it?"

"It's a bank deposit. It has your name and your brother's on it. He was holding it in his fist."

She stared at the paper and, lifting her eyes to Fargo, said, "You mean . . ." But she was not able to finish the sentence.

Fargo didn't say anything but watched the tears welling in her eyes. For some moments they stood there, the girl weeping, Fargo simply waiting.

Presently she looked down at the slip of paper again. "I don't understand. If he had our names on it, was even holding it in his hand, then why didn't he give it to me?"

Fargo looked at her quietly for a moment without speaking. And then he said simply, "But he did give it to you. You've got it."

Several moments passed while they stood there in the meadow with the sunlight waning.

"I just wish he had come home," she said.

"I think he did." And Fargo added, "He was a good man, John Logan."

She nodded, her head bowed. Then, looking up at him again with an odd look that transformed her completely, she said, "And so was Burl Boden, wouldn't you say?"

"I'd say they were one of a kind" the Trailsman answered simply.

"I was waiting for you," Fargo said as Sally stepped into the little clearing where he had camped outside Washing Springs.

"I know."

She was dressed in the lemon blouse he liked so much and tight riding pants that molded her hips and buttocks superbly.

For a moment they stood facing each other. It was just sundown of the day they'd arrived in Washing Springs. Frannie and Sally had taken rooms at the Buffalo Horn, Hank had repaired to the Good Times Saloon to catch up, as he'd put it. And Fargo, not one to favor indoor living, had camped a short way out of town. How she'd found him, he had no idea. But he'd known too that if she wanted him, she'd locate his camp.

After a moment Sally spoke. "Fargo, I've—I've never . . ."

"I know."

"I guess it shows, does it?"

"It's not something bad," he said mildly. "Only you have to start some time."

She took a step toward him. "I just don't want to spoil anything . . . I mean, for you."

"Why don't you let me be the judge of that," he said softly, and somehow they were suddenly standing very close together. In the next moment her lips were soft, like a butterfly on his. He circled her with his arms, as his erection drove between her tight legs.

"Open your legs," he whispered, prodding gently.

Suddenly she had spread her thighs and was on his rigid member. Her mouth pressed hard, and her tongue now darted into his mouth, searching his tongue. He felt her hands gripping his back, sliding down to his waist.

He looked down into the turmoil in her hazel eyes. She didn't move as he began unbuttoning the lemon-colored blouse—button by button, slowly, gently. He pushed the blouse back over her shoulders, down from her breasts, which sprang naked into the cool air—superbly curved with deep undersides and hard nipples pointing out to him. He pulled the blouse all the way off while she gasped, still looking into his eyes, her breath soaring. Next he reached down and unbuttoned her riding pants, slid them down

160

around her legs and, taking out his rigid member, placed it between her legs, over her downy vagina, which was still in her underpants. She sagged against him, her knees weak.

"Oh my God, ooooh, oh, my Fargo." Her breath washed the words into his lips as he kissed her again and then, lowering his head, found one high, hard nipple and took it in his mouth, teasing it with his circling tongue, biting it lightly and sucking.

She was gasping, hardly able to stand as he finished undressing her, while her hands were clutching at his trousers to undress him. In a moment he helped and they stood together in the moonlight totally naked, with his erection between her thighs, tight against her generous bush.

Easily, his hands slid slowly onto her breasts, then down to the full round smoothness of her abdomen to caress the dark full mound of wet hair.

In a moment he had pulled her onto his bed, lying on top of her, with his knees parting hers. "Draw your knees up and spread them," he said as he slipped his big hands under her quivering buttocks.

"Let me . . . Let me, Fargo . . ." And she was almost crying as she rose on her knees and, bending over him, took his huge maleness in her mouth and began to suck. Releasing it, she kissed its long, thick shaft and again went fully down on it, almost gagging.

"I wanted him like that first," she whispered as she lay down. "To kiss you there. Oh God, I've thought about it so very much!"

"Don't think now," he said. "Just let it happen."

And again he felt her fingers exploring him, cradling his balls, squeezing, stroking his great shaft. And now he spun her onto her back as she gasped. "Oh . . . yes, Fargo . . . yes, yes, yes . . . Please now, please now, dear Fargo . . ." And as he sank his maleness into her, forcing her open to receive it, she cried out, "Help me, Fargo . . . I want it so, every inch, every sweet inch . . . Aieeee . . . oh, oh, oh, oh, oh . . ." And as he began pumping she was matching his rhythm, squeezing her legs, her buttocks thrashing on the bed as she dug her heels into the ground, bucking him, riding into oblivion as they both exploded together with her screams piercing the air all the way to the climax of the wild throbbing that engulfed them both.

Her screams subsided into gasps and heavy breathing. They were both running with water, lying together, she with her legs still around him, trying to suck him into her even then.

He lay on the grass beside the bedroll, his arm around her, while they both looked up at the starry sky. Neither noticed until then that there had been a change in the light.

In a little while she spoke without turning her head toward him, speaking up to the stars.

"I want to be with you, Fargo . . . but, but I

know you want to be free." She turned to him then. "I just wanted you to know that."

"Will you go back to Willow Falls?"

"I must tell my brother what's happened."

"Of course."

"And you, Fargo?"

"Well," he said after a moment. "Like you, I'm also looking for someone."

"I hope you find the person."

"I will," he said softly, remembering the promise he had made when he was eighteen and had looked down at the dead bodies that had only a moment before been his family.

The girl beside him sensed something, but she didn't speak. She reached out and touched his hand. "All these years of wanting, and I found you, Fargo. And now you'll go away."

"I could never forget a girl like you," Fargo said, rising up on his elbow and looking down at her.

She was smiling, even though her eyes were watering. "I'd like to believe that," she said.

"It's true."

"But you'll still be around for a while, anyway," she said, and he caught the teasing in her voice and her eyes.

"How do you know that?"

She had reached down and was fondling his organ, which had become immediately stiff. "I won't bother to convince you," she said, "but him."

And still gripping him, she pulled Fargo over

on top of her, guiding his enormous organ into her soaking bush of dark brown hair, while her heels dug into the bedding and she rose, arching so he thrust himself up into the very center of her body; and as they pulsed together he felt every part of himself throbbing with impossible joy, the only true ecstasy. This time they found a closer rhythm, and it lasted longer.

Long after they were finished and lay side by side, Sally said, "You're an excellent teacher, Mr. Fargo."

And Fargo replied, "There's only an excellent teacher when there's an excellent pupil, Miss Logan. You should know that from your school."

"I know it now," she whispered, turning to him yet once more.

Fargo was in no hurry to leave.

LOOKING FORWARD!

The following is the opening section
from the next novel in the exciting
Trailsman series from Signet:

The Trailsman #28
HOSTAGE TRAIL

High in the Montana wilderness in
the mid-1860s, deep in the heart
of hostile Blackfoot country.

Skye Fargo ducked his head again into the icy
water. He held it under the surface for almost
thirty seconds. Then he brought it up, shaking it
and blowing like a grizzly who had just missed a
trout. Despite the late October chill, he had
thrown off his deerskin shirt, revealing muscles
that stood out like mole tunnels. They rippled
and flashed in the sunlight as he pulled back from
the riverbank. Sitting back, he gazed about him,
his lake-blue eyes taking in his surroundings with
a commanding, eaglelike ferocity.

He had hoped the stream's icy shock would
clear his head of the bourbon that still fogged his
senses. It had. The mean little town he'd left five

miles back along the trail had boasted little more than a ramshackle hotel, a saloon and a general store. The whores ran the hotel, the saloon-keeper ran the whores, and the owner of the general store owned them all. The town was a festering sore at the juncture of two mountain steams and existed for the sole purpose of giving the men of Fort Ellis a place to blow their pay. Fargo had spent a full night in the place, boozing and carousing.

But that had not been Fargo's purpose in coming to that town high in the Montana wilderness—and his brief visit there had meant, for him, the end of one more fruitless quest.

He had found the man he was tracking, all right. He was a sleazy swamper who matched in some particulars the description of one of the three men he sought. But this runt, it turned out, wasn't one of them. He had the pedigree, sure enough, but his age and history had not been right. Matching him bottle for bottle the night before, Fargo had determined this without a doubt.

Meanwhile, the swamper had never realized that he was drinking with a man who had journeyed a long way to find and kill him. And if Fargo had not checked the swamper's story as carefully as he had, the little no-account might well have been found this morning facedown in an outhouse, his mouth stuffed with shit.

Fargo got to his full six feet, shook his head like a great cat, then combed back his unruly black hair with long, talonlike fingers. His deerskin shirt was lying on the grass. He plucked it up and ducked into it, his massive shoulders filling it out impressively. Turning, he strode back to his Ovaro pinto and checked the cinch buckles. He was about to swing into his saddle when he heard two sharp screams.

In this pristine wilderness—where the chatter of chipmunks and echoing birds were all he heard for hours on end—the screams riveted Fargo. Then came another scream. And another. They came from two women. He was sure of it. And they were close by, just beyond a wooded ridge ahead of him.

Fargo pulled out his huge Colt and loped noiselessly up onto the ridge and into the pines crowning it. Breaking out a moment later, he saw the river looping lazily back around the ridge, and crowding close upon it, just below him, a grassy bank.

On the bank two Indian girls were fighting off a couple of troopers. The squaws had obviously come to the stream to bathe and had been caught as naked as on the day God made them, their deerskin skirts and blouses piled neatly beneath a nearby pine. They were considerably smaller than their burly attackers, but they were putting up a fierce struggle—so fierce they were no longer wasting any more energy screaming. The troopers—as inept as they were rotten—were having a difficult time peeling off their britches and holding on to their thrashing victims at the same time.

Keeping to the ridge, Fargo worked his way around behind the struggling foursome, then angled down the steep slope until he was within a few yards of them. One of the troopers had managed to rid himself of his britches by this time and had cuffed his Indian woman into a sullen submission. The other trooper was not as efficient. He was being beaten back steadily by the furious Indian squaw twisting and gyrating wildly under him.

Both squaws saw Fargo approaching. But one look at Fargo's angry face and they knew enough not to give him away. Fargo stopped behind the trooper without his britches and brought around the barrel of his Colt, slamming him on the side of his head. The force of the blow drove him violently sideways. He stumbled groggily, lost his balance, then collapsed facedown on the grass, unconscious.

The other trooper heard the commotion and started to turn. Fargo stepped closer, held the revolver up to his ear, cocked and fired. The round whined off harmlessly across the river, but the Colt's thunderous detonation shattered the trooper's eardrum. With a startled howl of pain, the trooper spun away from him, his hand clapped to his ear. As he moaned in agony Fargo followed after him and clubbed him senseless to the ground.

He returned to the squaws and helped them to their feet. "Get your clothes on," he told them, pointing to their neat pile of clothing under the pine, "and vamoose!"

They did not understand his words, but his intent was obvious. Thanking him with grateful nods, they darted over to the pine and hurriedly began to dress.

They were Blackfeet. Fargo knew this from the black-dyed moccasins they hurriedly stepped into as well as from the dark symmetry of their faces—and the gleaming, satiny finish to their supple, well-proportioned bodies. The Blackfeet were a handsome tribe, and these two squaws were no exception. Neither of them could have been more than sixteen years old, but Fargo had no difficulty understanding why the sight of such lush ripeness had driven the two troopers to attack them. There was nothing even remotely as appealing waiting for them in the town Fargo had left that morning.

But that sure as hell didn't excuse the bastards. Just made it more understandable.

Without a word to Fargo, the squaws finished dressing and vanished into the thick woodland bordering the river. Fargo approached the two troopers and nudged them with his boot to see if they were coming out of it. They did not respond. Fargo realized he might have killed the first one, he had swung with such enthusiasm. But he didn't care all that much. If a Blackfoot brave had caught him and his partner attacking those two squaws, they would both be dead now, the tops of their skulls a bloody, hairless mess. And it would have served them right.

Fargo went back for his pinto. When he returned, the two soldiers were regaining consciousness. One of them—the skinnier of the two—was holding the side of his face, the other his shattered ear. When they saw Fargo leading his pinto toward them, they scrambled to their feet. Neither man was a pleasure to contemplate. The trooper Fargo had struck on the face was in his late twenties—a sorry-looking bag of bones with crooked teeth and close-set eyes.

His companion—still naked from the waist down—was considerably older and fatter. He had a porcine face, a whiskey-red nose and a puddinglike gut that sagged down over his genitals. A glowering meanness hung over him. He looked with pure, undiluted hatred at Fargo.

"Get your britches on, you poor sad sonofabitch," Fargo told the fat one. "I'm taking you and your buddy back to the fort."

"I'll get you for this," the trooper replied, "and don't think I won't."

"Sure, you will. Now pull on them britches, or I'll make you march into Fort Ellis without them."

"Damn you to hell!" the fellow seethed, as he hurried over to retrieve his pants. "Who in hell invited you to this party?"

"I invited myself."

"Them was just redskin heathens!" he cried, pulling on his britches. "What are you anyway, a damned Indian lover?"

"Sure. Why not? I'm part Indian. And for white bastards like you, I got little patience."

The lean one had said nothing. He had contented himself with glaring at Fargo. Now he slouched closer to his companion and licked his lips. He looked about ready to spring. "C'mon, Pete!" he said to his companion, "we can take this sonofabitch! There's two of us and only one of him."

Fargo lifted his Colt and fired. The round burned past the lean one's cheek. Fargo fired again. This time the slug exploded inches from his feet. The trooper jumped back, his eyes wide in sudden panic.

"Forget it, Slim," said Pete, hastily buckling his belt. "We'll get the bastard later."

Fargo waited until they were ready, then swung into his saddle, his Colt leveled on the two men.

"Start walking," he told them. "I'll be right behind you."

"But we got horses," protested Slim.

"I'll send someone back for them. I want you both to walk. Do you good to sweat a little. The first one tries anything'll get a piece of hot lead up his ass. Let's go!"

Without a backward glance the two would-be rapists started for Fort Ellis.

Less than an hour later the sorry caravan moved through the post's gate. As it closed a number of armed troopers hurried over to surround Fargo and the two men.

"Stand back," Fargo told them, "or I'll ventilate your buddies."

The troopers fell warily back and Fargo kept his two captives heading toward the headquarters building. Dismounting in front of it, he herded them inside. The sergeant at the desk jumped to his feet at Fargo's abrupt entry. But one look at the two men Fargo was covering and his belligerence faded.

"All right, mister," he asked Fargo in a kind of weary resignation, "what have these two no-accounts been up to this time?"

"Caught them raping a couple of Blackfoot Indian squaws."

The sergeant—a burly Irishman—turned swiftly, knocked on the commanding officer's door, then stepped inside. A moment later a visibly disturbed C.O. hurried out of his office, the sergeant on his heels.

Glancing at Fargo, the officer asked unhappily, "You're sure they were Blackfeet?"

"I'm sure."

"Damn!" The officer turned to the sergeant. "Throw these two in the stockade, Sergeant. I've had enough from them. This time it will be a full court-martial! I am throwing the book at them!"

The sergeant nodded, strode to the door, flung it open and ordered a Corporal Riley to report on the double. While they waited for the corporal, Fargo explained to the sergeant where he had caught the two men and suggested he send some troopers for their mounts. A moment later a freckle-faced redhead not much older than eighteen arrived and escorted his two prisoners from the building.

As soon as they had left, the commanding officer introduced himself. "I am Captain George Smollett," he said, shaking Fargo's hand. "And who might you be?"

"Skye Fargo."

"Come into my office, Fargo. Join me in a drink and tell me what happened."

Fargo followed the captain into his office and sat down in a chair beside the man's desk. The captain was an impressive-looking officer, well over six feet with a thick shock of dark hair and a handlebar mustache. His jaw looked as solid as a block of granite and his handsome dark eyes gleamed out from under craggy brows.

As soon as he saw Fargo was comfortable the captain reached into his desk's bottom drawer and pulled forth a recently opened bottle of whiskey. He almost filled completely the two large beakers he produced from the same drawer. It was obvious to Fargo that Captain Smollett was a man who thought large in all things.

Thanking the captain, Fargo took the glass of whiskey. The two men saluted each other, then drank. Wiping his mouth with the back of his hand, Fargo leaned back in his chair. It was already getting chilly in this high country and the whiskey sent a deep, much-needed warmth coursing through his long frame. "Looks like you've already had trouble with them two troopers," he remarked.

"That I have indeed! Worthless, both of them."

"What were they doing out there?"

"My Shoshone scouts have heard rumors there were Blood Blackfeet in the area. Seems they are feeling pressure from the Teton Sioux, who are encroaching on their traditional hunting grounds. Those two troopers were on patrol. They were supposed to be on the lookout for any sign of Bloods near the fort and report back at once."

"They found Blackfeet, all right," Fargo commented, finishing his whiskey. "They just figured to try out the merchandise before reporting back here."

Smollett shook his head in disgust and refilled Fargo's glass.

Fargo said, "I reckon you can imagine the story them two young squaws will be telling when they get back to them Blackfoot lodges. Should sure as hell stir things up, like a grizzly in a beehive. Might even give them the idea to come looking for some army horseflesh they could use against the Sioux. If it's one thing them Blackfeet like, it's a good excuse to cut loose."

"I'm afraid you're right, Fargo. They won't hesitate to attack a white man if they think they can get away with it. I've already doubled the sentries and increased the scope and size of my patrols. Now, thanks to those damn troopers, we will have to proceed on the assumption we are in hostile Indian country."

The captain shook his head and refilled his own glass.

"I'd rather handle Crow than Blackfeet," he commented thoughtfully. "The Crow you can bargain with. They are a shrewd, opportunistic tribe. And luckily, Washakie has always kept the Shoshones on our side. But the Blackfeet are a murderous lot with long, long memories. They will not soon forget this outrage."

Fargo finished his drink and got to his feet. "Thanks for the drink," he said. "Time I saw to my horse and headed out. White trouble I came looking for. Trouble with the Blackfeet I'd just as soon pass up."

"Hold on there, Fargo," the captain said, getting to his feet also. "I was hoping you would stay with us awhile—join me for dinner this evening, at least. It's army cooking, but I am blessed with an excellent cook."

Fargo considered a moment. He liked the captain and it wouldn't be polite to rush off. Besides, a good meal on clean china appealed to him. He shrugged and smiled. "Suits me, Captain," he said. "Do you think you could scare up some quarters for me? I'll need it to clean up and maybe grab a little shut-eye. I got precious little last night."

The captain walked with Fargo to the door. "Consider it done, Fargo. My sergeant will take care of you. I'll expect you at seven. But come early and we'll open a fresh bottle."

The fresh bottle contained fine Kentucky bourbon and Fargo found himself drinking it with the captain and three of his guests, two brothers and a tall young blonde in her early twenties. The brothers were Karl and Emil Borglund, the girl's name was Kristen Swenson. Kristen was Karl's fiancée, and if Fargo ever found himself forced to settle down with one woman, he decided he could not do much better than this clear-eyed blonde standing before him.

She was astonishingly beautiful, her cleanly sculpted features set off by her high cheekbones. Her lips were full and passionate, her teeth like pearls. Rather than decorously parting her hair in the middle and wearing it in a bun behind her head, she allowed her long blond curls to cascade saucily down her back. Perhaps an inch or so taller than her fiancé, she was dressed almost formally in a long green gown with plenty of lace at her throat, the bodice fitted over a corset that must have reduced her waist to less than twenty inches. Frilly petticoats peeked out from under her long green skirt, but something in her frank blue eyes told Fargo that under all that finery, she was bare-bottomed. There was indeed a hint of rebelliousness about her, and at times Fargo saw subtle indications of her impatience with the two men at her side.

Her fiancé, Karl, was the younger of the two brothers. His dark, clean-cut features were handsome enough to attract and hold a woman as beautiful as Kristen, but there was a weakness about his mouth that bothered Fargo, and a bluster that soon made those around him edgy. He was slim, just under six feet tall, tanned and fit enough looking, as was his brother, who appeared to be about three years older. Except in their manner, both men resembled each other closely; it had been apparent from the moment Fargo entered the captain's quarters that they were brothers.

As they and the captain had explained to Fargo, the three of them were on their way to Karl's ranch along the Canadian border. About ten years earlier their parents had established their own ranch not too far from where Karl had just finished building his own place. The two brothers had journeyed all the way back to Illinois in order to escort Kristen to Karl's ranch, where she and Karl would be married.

After the introductions, Karl did the most talking, while Fargo nursed his drink, hung back and took everything in. He soon found he did not like Karl. The young man was a braggart, while his older brother, Emil, seemed concerned only with placating him. That was a shame, for Karl badly needed curbing. His most annoying trait was expressing, on almost any pretext, his massive and overwhelming contempt for the Indians, whom he considered the most miserable and benighted of creatures.

Captain Smollett tried to balance the view somewhat. As he was able to point out, he had had many years on the frontier and had met many Indians who had shown great courage and even greater loyalty to their own people and even to whites they had befriended. But the captain's fair-minded comments had little effect on Karl, who swept them aside with scorn. After Fargo had taken about all of this he could stomach, he took a step closer to Karl and cleared his throat. Karl turned to him expectantly.

"You don't seem to have much respect for the Indian," Fargo commented.

"Why should I?" Karl demanded. "They are ignorant aborigines, savages without culture. They will drink themselves into oblivion."

"They are all worthless?"

"Yes. And cowards to boot. There is entirely too much fear of them. It is generated, I am sure, by those who know nothing at all about their true nature. They are a filthy, immoral lot—and the sooner they are wiped out, the better it will be for all of us."

"All Indians, every one of them?"

"Yes."

"Even those whites with Indian blood?" Fargo asked mildly.

"You mean half-breeds?" Karl spat contemptuously. "Why, Mr. Fargo! In truth, they are far worse than a full-blooded Indian. I have never met a mixed blood who was worth a damn."

"That so?" Fargo commented mildly.

The captain tried to say something, but Fargo smiled at him and waved him off.

"Surely," said Karl, "you are aware of that,

Mr. Fargo. You look like a man who's had plenty of experience in these matters. Am I not right?"

"That's true. I have had considerable experience with Indians. But you see, I am of mixed blood myself. My mother had a goodly portion of Indian blood running in her veins." Fargo smiled coldly. "She boasted of it, and I am proud of it."

Karl swallowed and took a short step back, his face pale. "Well, surely, Mr. Fargo, you realize I had no way of knowing that. My remarks were made in general; I had no one specifically in mind."

"I am glad no offense was intended," Fargo said mildly, a steel edge to his words nevertheless.

Karl immediately changed the topic, then found some excuse for moving off with his brother. Kristen did not move off with them, however. Instead, she glanced boldly at Fargo, the ghost of a smile playing about her lovely mouth, as if she understood perfectly what Fargo thought of her fiancé—and agreed.

The two commissioned officers who assisted Smollett in running the post—First Lieutenant Mulroy and Second Lieutenant Hesse—arrived at that moment, dissipating the awkwardness that had descended on the room's occupants. A moment later, the steward announced that the dinner was ready and a grateful Captain Smollett showed them to the table.

As the captain had promised, the meal was excellent. Venison stew started things off, to be followed by a platter full of inch-thick steaks smothered in onions, another platter containing baked potatoes and thick slabs of still-warm bread, with plenty of freshly salted butter to spread on it. Strawberry shortcake was served as dessert, and the coffee that finished the meal was hearty enough to put hair on a cannonball.

Retiring to the living room afterward, they were served an after-dinner wine. As soon as all the guests had their glasses in hand, the captain raised his glass and proposed a toast.

"To Karl and Kristen," he said. "May they reach their new home safely and have a full, rich life as man and wife."

Kristen accepted this toast with a flashing smile and a slight blush. Karl strutted. About some things Karl was no fool. He knew what a prize he was about to possess.

As Fargo lowered his glass Captain Smollett looked at him and cleared his throat. At once the others all turned to stare at Fargo also.

"Mr. Fargo," Smollett said, "you see before you in these three young people the future of this country. It is the young and vibrant citizens such as these who brave the wilderness and plant the seeds of civilization in this great country. It is they who will claim it for all of us. Do you agree?"

Fargo shrugged. "I reckon that's what's coming, Captain, sure enough."

"And that means ridding this land of those godless heathen," said Karl. He had regained his composure now and was not going to back down one little bit when it came to his convictions. "Do you approve of that, Mr. Fargo?"

"You mean do I approve replacing the cowardly aborigines with right-thinking Christians?"

"That's right."

"What Christian would not?"

"Precisely."

"Then you will help us?" asked Kristen.

Fargo glanced at the captain, a frown on his face. "I don't understand, Captain," he replied. "Why are you all gunning me with your eyes? What's Miss Kristen mean? Help in what?"

"I was hoping," the captain explained, "that you might consent to serve as their guide through the Indian country."

"You see," broke in Emil, the older brother, "we went back to Illinois by way of Canada. It was Karl's wish, however, to return by this route. Unfortunately, the Indians have been acting up, so after this unfortunate incident with the Blackfeet, the captain feels if would be helpful if you accompanied us."

"Enlistments have been falling off," went on Smollett. "I simply do not have the men to escort them. I am lucky to have the number I do to man this post. And you saw today how reliable most of those men are."

"So you want me to take them through Indian country."

"I think you're the man who could do it."

"I think so too," said Kristen.

"I wish I shared your confidence," Fargo told them. "After what happened today, I am sure the Blackfeet will be looking for chances to punish anyone who emerges from this post."

"Perhaps," said Smollett, "but do not forget, Fargo. It was you who saved those Blackfeet squaws. Surely that will count for something with the Blackfeet if they do intercept you."

"Probably, but I wouldn't put too much faith in that, Captain," Fargo said. "I suggest these three wait until the Bloods leave this country. This is just a large raiding party. Once they get their fill of Crow horses and count enough coup, they'll move out."

"But they will still be between us and the border," said Emil. "Is that not true?"

"There is a likelihood of that, yes."

"Well I for one do not intend to spend the winter here," announced Karl. "I intend to spend it on the border in my new home with Kristen. And she is just as anxious as I to move north. If you will not take us, Fargo, we will set out without you."

"Please," said Kristen to Fargo, "do come with

us. I would feel so much safer if you were with us."

Karl spun on the girl. "Kristen! Do not humble yourself. We do not need Mr. Fargo. Emil and I are perfectly capable of seeing you through Indian country. You will be as safe with us as you would be with him."

"Of course, Karl," she said, as soothingly as if she were addressing a pampered child, "but Mr. Fargo would be such a great help, we might even get to our new home sooner, before winter closes in."

Emil spoke up then. "We know it is a great imposition, Mr. Fargo, but the captain assures us you know the territory."

Fargo shrugged. He had already made up his mind. To leave Kristen in the hands of this fool fiancé of hers would be tantamount to throwing her to the wolves. "Yes," he replied. "I do know the land. And like you, I don't fancy spending the winter in this fort. It doesn't matter to me which way I go at the moment. North or south. One direction is as good as another."

"Then you'll come with us?" Kristen asked, eyes alight.

Fargo looked at her and smiled. "Yes," he said.

"Thank you very much," Kristen said, returning Fargo's smile.

Karl had no choice now but to make the best of it. "All right, then, Mr. Fargo," he said curtly.

"We shall be pleased to have your company. But we pull out tomorrow, first thing in the morning. Can you be ready by then?"

"I can."

"Good." He turned to Kristen and Emil. "Come. We have some packing to do."

As soon as the door closed behind them, Fargo turned to the captain and his two officers. "I don't mind Emil and that girl," he said, "but Karl is going to be trouble—bad trouble. Someone ought to take him across his knees and whale the tar out of him."

"It is too late for that, I am afraid," admitted the captain.

The other two officers nodded solemnly.

"Maybe it is," said Fargo, "but if that pompous ass doesn't start growing up soon, the Blackfeet might do far worse than paddle his ass."

Fargo finished his wine. At the moment he would have preferred something stronger, but judging from what lay ahead of him, he would be needing a clear head in the morning. "Good night, gentlemen," he said, heading for the door. His hand on the knob, he looked back at the captain, smiling somewhat ruefully. "And I thank you for a most excellent dinner, Captain—if not for this chore you just handed me."

The captain shrugged. "What choice did I have, Fargo? Answer me honestly now. If you were me, would you not do all you could to keep such a girl from being escorted through hostile Indian country solely in the care of that fiancé of hers and his brother?"

"Hell, why do you think I am going with them?"

With a casual salute, Fargo closed the door and headed for his quarters.

Someone was starting a Mexican revolution just outside Fargo's door. Awake instantly, Fargo grabbed the Colt under his pillow and sat bolt upright. A shot blasted from the other side of the door. Then a boot struck it. The wood splintered. Another boot slammed into it. The lock broke free and the door swung wide. Into the room rushed Pete, the trooper whose eardrum Fargo had shattered earlier that day. He was brandishing a six-gun.

Behind Pete on the barracks floor, a trooper lay faceup, blood pooling under his head. As Fargo brought up his own Colt Pete dived to one side, firing at Fargo as he did so. The slug whined off the bunk and ricocheted into the ceiling. Fargo rolled off the bed as Pete fired again. This time the round exploded into Fargo's pillow, filling the air with feathers.

Fargo swung himself in under the bed, came out on the other side and burst up from the floor, his Colt thundering twice. Both slugs caught Pete in the chest. Two neat black holes appeared on his shirtfront. He slammed back against the wall, the Colt still in his hand. He fired a third time, the round plunging into the floor at Fargo's feet.

Fargo twisted the six-gun from his hand and swung it like a club. The barrel caught Pete on the tip of his jaw. There was a sickening crack as his jawbone broke and he went tumbling back into a corner. For a second or two he remained upright, his back to the wall, his shattered jaw hanging loosely. Then he just toppled forward heavily, like a downed fir tree, and crashed facedown onto the floor. Fargo stepped back as a puddle of blood began to spread from under Pete's shattered face. Two large, untidy holes stared up at him from the back of his shirt, and from both holes came a steady, pulsing stream of blood.

Fargo reckoned Pete was dead or close enough, and lowered his Colt.

Glancing up, he saw armed troopers rushing through the barracks toward his room. The wounded trooper on the floor outside Fargo's door began to stir fitfully. Two troopers helped him to his feet as a third rushed past them into Fargo's room.

The trooper pulled hastily back when he saw the unconscious Pete. He swallowed and took a deep breath, then looked at Fargo.

"Is he dead?"

Fargo walked over to Pete's still form and nudged him over with his boot. Pete came to rest with his face up, his wide eyes staring sightlessly up at the ceiling. Fargo looked back at the trooper.

"He's dead, all right. Where's his buddy—Slim?"

"They both broke out of the stockade to get you, mister. But Slim didn't like the odds. He's gone over the wall."

Fargo looked back down at the dead trooper. It was too bad Pete had not done the same thing. "Drag the sonofabitch the hell out of here and get me a new pillow," Fargo growled, sitting wearily down on the edge of his bed. "What's a man got to do to get a good night's sleep around here?"

The trooper hurried to do Fargo's bidding, and a few minutes later, with a fresh pillow under his head—and under that a reloaded Colt—Fargo was once again sound asleep.

JOIN THE TRAILSMAN READER'S PANEL
AND PREVIEW NEW BOOKS

If you're a reader of TRAILSMAN, New American Library wants to bring you more of the type of books you enjoy. For this reason we're asking you to join TRAILSMAN Reader's Panel, to preview new books, so we can learn more about your reading tastes.

Please fill out and mail today. Your comments are appreciated.

1. The title of the last paperback book I bought was: _____
_____

2. How many paperback books have you bought for yourself in the last six months?
   ☐ 1 to 3   ☐ 4 to 6   ☐ 10 to 20   ☐ 21 or more

3. What other paperback fiction have you read in the past six months? Please list titles:_____
_____
_____

4. I usually buy my books at: (Check One or more)
   ☐ Book Store   ☐ Newsstand   ☐ Discount Store
   ☐ Supermarket   ☐ Drug Store   ☐ Department Store
   ☐ Other (Please specify)_____

5. I listen to radio regularly: (Check One)   ☐ Yes   ☐ No
   My favorite station is:_____
   I usually listen to radio (Circle One or more)   On way to work /
   During the day / Coming home from work / In the evening

6. I read magazines regularly: (Check One)   ☐ Yes   ☐ No
   My favorite magazine is:_____

7. I read a newspaper regularly: (Check One)   ☐ Yes   ☐ No
   My favorite newspaper is:_____
   My favorite section of the newspaper is:_____

For our records, we need this information from all our Reader's Panel Members.
NAME:_____
ADDRESS:_____ZIP_____
TELEPHONE: Area Code (   ) Number_____

8. (Check One)   ☐ Male   ☐ Female

9. Age (Check One)   ☐ 17 and under   ☐ 18 to 34
   ☐ 35 to 49   ☐ 50 to 64   ☐ 65 and over

10. Education (Check One)
    ☐ Now in high school   ☐ Graduated high school
    ☐ Now in college   ☐ Completed some college
    ☐ Graduated college

As our special thanks to all members of our Reader's Panel, we'll send a free gift of special interest to readers of THE TRAILSMAN.

Thank you. Please mail this in today.

NEW AMERICAN LIBRARY
PROMOTION DEPARTMENT
1633 BROADWAY
NEW YORK, NY 10019

SIGNET Westerns You'll Enjoy

(0451)

- [ ] **CIMARRON #1: CIMARRON AND THE HANGING JUDGE** by Leo P. Kelley.
  (120582—$2.50)*
- [ ] **CIMARRON #2: CIMARRON RIDES THE OUTLAW TRAIL** by Leo P. Kelley.
  (120590—$2.50)*
- [ ] **CIMARRON #3: CIMARRON AND THE BORDER BANDITS** by Leo P. Kelley.
  (122518—$2.50)*
- [ ] **CIMARRON #4: CIMARRON IN THE CHEROKEE STRIP** by Leo P. Kelley.
  (123441—$2.50)*
- [ ] **CIMARRON #5: CIMARRON AND THE ELK SOLDIERS** by Leo P. Kelley.
  (124898—$2.50)*
- [ ] **CIMARRON #6: CIMARRON AND THE BOUNTY HUNTERS** by Leo P. Kelley.
  (125703—$2.50)*
- [ ] **CIMARRON #7: CIMARRON AND THE HIGH RIDER** by Leo P. Kelley.
  (126866—$2.50)*
- [ ] **CIMARRON #8: CIMARRON IN NO MAN'S LAND** by Leo P. Kelley.
  (128230—$2.50)*
- [ ] **LUKE SUTTON: OUTLAW** by Leo P. Kelley.   (115228—$1.95)*
- [ ] **LUKE SUTTON: GUNFIGHTER** by Leo P. Kelley.   (122836—$2.25)*
- [ ] **LUKE SUTTON: INDIAN FIGHTER** by Leo P. Kelley. (124553—$2.25)*
- [ ] **THE HALF-BREED** by Mick Clumpner.   (112814—$1.95)*
- [ ] **MASSACRE AT THE GORGE** by Mick Clumpner.   (117433—$1.95)*

  *Prices slightly higher in Canada

**Buy them at your local
bookstore or use coupon
on next page for ordering.**

Wild Westerns by Warren T. Longtree